SAPP

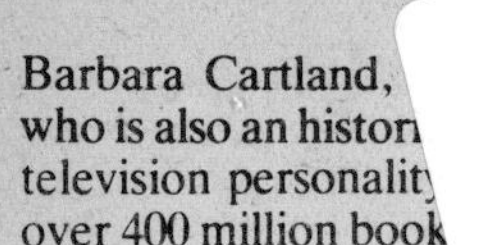

Barbara Cartland, ... st,
who is also an histori... d
television personalit... d
over 400 million book...

She has also had ... has
written four autobiog... graphies of her
mother and that of her ... Cartland, who was the
first Member of Parliam... be killed in the last war. This book
has a preface by Sir Winston Churchill and has just been republished with an introduction by Sir Arthur Bryant.

"Love at the Helm" a novel written with the help and inspiration of the late Earl Mountbatten of Burma, Uncle of His Royal Highness The Duke of Edinburgh, is being sold for the Mountbatten Memorial Trust.

Miss Cartland in 1978 sang an Album of Love Songs with the Royal Philharmonic Orchestra.

In 1976 by writing twenty-one books, she broke the world record and has continued for the following nine years with 24, 20, 23, 24, 24, 25, 23, 25 and 26. In the Guinness Book of Records she is listed as the world's top-selling author.

In private life Barbara Cartland, who is a Dame of Grace of the Order of St. John of Jerusalem, Chairman of the St. John Council in Hertfordshire and Deputy President of the St. John Ambulance Brigade, has fought for better conditions and salaries for Midwives and Nurses.

She has championed the cause for old people, had the law altered regarding gypsies and founded the first Romany Gypsy camp in the world.

Barbara Cartland is deeply interested in Vitamin therapy, and is President of the National Association for Health.

Barbara Cartland's book "Getting Older, Growing Younger", and her cookery book "The Romance of Food" have been published in Great Britain, the U.S.A., and in other parts of the world.

She has also written a Children's Pop-Up Book entitled "Princess to the Rescue."

Eagle Moss (Patrick Cavendish) is bringing out a hardback book by Barbara Cartland every fortnight at £1.95. Beautifully bound in red and gold leather and it will make a Barbara Cartland library.

By the same author in Pan Books

Alone and Afraid
Look with Love
Love Comes West
Love is a Gamble
Safe at Last
Temptation for a Teacher
A Victory for Love
The Secret of the Mosque
Haunted
A Dream in Spain
The Love Trap
An Angel Runs Away
Love Joins the Clans
Lovers in Lisbon

BARBARA CARTLAND

SAPPHIRES IN SIAM

Pan Original
Pan Books London and Sydney

First published 1987 by Pan Books Ltd,
Cavaye Place, London SW10 9PG
9 8 7 6 5 4 3 2 1

ISBN 0 330 29766 X
Printed and bound in Great Britain by
Collins, Glasgow

DEDICATION

Dedicated to Ankana Gilwee, who is a very important and charming part of the best hotel in the world – which is the fabulous Oriental in Bangkok.

AUTHOR'S NOTE

When I visited Thailand for the fourth time I went to Chiang Mai in the North, and Pattaya in the South.

In the popular sea resort which had once been a small fishing village, I found an ancient, unlisted Temple on a hill above the bay, exactly as I have described it in this novel.

Thailand is the only Buddhist country I have visited which sticks small specks of gold leaf on their Holy images.

Much of the authentic information in this book comes from a very interesting description of the Duke of Sutherland's voyage to Siam and Malaya in 1889.

The Duke's party was received by King Chulalongkorn and they dined in state in his Palace.

There were no *punkas* in Siam, but attendants in crimson costumes waved large feather fans over the heads of the guests, while a native band played Siamese music interspersed with a selection from "The Bohemian Girl", and "Faust".

Last Year I found the newly gilt Palace in Bangkok breathtakingly beautiful, the Oriental Hotel the finest hotel in the East, and Pattaya very exciting.

Chapter One
1898

The Marquis of Vale lay with closed eyes and knew he was bored.

Bored with the softness of the bed, the airlessness of the room, and the fragrance of tuberoses which were supposed to arouse passion.

He was bored too, with the warm, clinging creature lying close to him.

It was not unusual for the Marquis to be bored.

But on this occasion, when it was only the second time he had been in bed with Lady Sybil Westoak, his boredom had come upon him unprecedentedly quickly.

The trouble, the Marquis reflected, was that nothing that happened had any originality about it.

He was able to predict at the beginning of the evening exactly what would be said and what would happen.

Looking back over the last dozen of his love-affairs, he found there was a uniformity about them.

This inevitably made him bored long before the lady in question realised what was happening.

It was not surprising that the Marquis expected each of the women to whom he made love to have an individuality of her own.

All the landmarks in his life to date had been strangely unexpected.

He had entered the Army when he left Oxford and proved himself a good soldier and an outstanding commander, especially on the battle-field.

He had however, because of his strong personality and a talent for diplomacy, been sent to India as an *Aide-de-Camp* to the Viceroy.

While he was enjoying the East as a member of the Raj he had unexpectedly come into a huge fortune through his materlan grand-father.

On an impulse to escape from the pomp and conventions of his social life and his duties in India, he had resigned from the Army, and started to travel.

This had brought him in touch with all sorts of strange people, unusual religions and at times, into considerable danger.

When his father died he had inherited the Marquisate, again unexpectedly, owing to the death of his elder brother on the battle field.

This resulted in him finding himself lionised in the very sophisticated and amusing Society headed by the Prince of Wales.

It was only to be expected that he would be *persona grata* at Marlborough House.

It was no less inevitable that every woman who met him had a glint in her eye which was obviously an invitation.

At first the Marquis was pleasantly intrigued, finding the English Ladies of Quality very different from the women with whom he had associated on his travels.

But as somebody has said cynically: 'All cats are grey in the dark', and he soon found a sameness about his successive *affaires de coeur* which made him yawn.

What he really enjoyed, if he was honest, was the preliminary chase.

It gave him the same feeling of excitement and achievement as when he had climbed in the Himalayas, or of finally being a victor when some lovely woman surrendered herself to him.

Unfortunately, it did not happen like that.

Lady Sybil had stalked him as if he was a stag for two months before he finally succumbed to her insistence.

She was exceedingly beautiful.

He had thought when he first saw her come into the Ball-Room at Marlborough House after he had enjoyed an intimate dinner with the Prince and Princess of Wales, that she was exceptional.

When finally it was he who succumbed rather than she who surrendered he found that she was no different from the other women he had left unhappy or affronted over the past years.

There was no doubt that Lady Sybil was very lovely.

She had the beauty of a Greek goddess and her hair was the colour of the sky at dawn.

But there was nothing behind the transparency of her blue eyes and she never said anything that he could remember afterwards.

Their love-making had been satisfactory – he could not deny that.

At the same time, he knew that he wanted something more than physical satisfaction.

What that was he could not explain even to himself.

He threw back the lace-edged sheet, and as he started to get out of the bed Lady Sybil gave a little cry of anguish.

"You are not leaving me, Osmond?"

"It is time I went home."

"But it is still quite early! How can I lose you?"

The Marquis did not answer, and she went on, her hands caressing him:

"No one could be a more wonderful lover, and it is marvellous that as Edward is away, we can be together again tomorrow night."

The Marquis knew that from his point of view that was improbable, but he was too tactful to say so.

Only with difficulty, because Lady Sybil was clinging to him, did he manage to get to his feet.

She threw herself petulantly back against the pillows saying:

"I cannot think why you must leave me when there is no chance of anybody stirring in the house until five o'clock."

"You forget I have to be home before my servants are awake," the Marquis replied.

Lady Sybil laughed.

"They must be used by this time to your coming in with the dawn! But, darling I will let you go now if you promise you will dine here tomorrow night."

She paused a moment, and then continued:

"I shall see you at luncheon, as we are both invited to Devonshire House."

The Marquis, dressing himself quickly and deftly, thought that the only redeeming feature at luncheon would be the Duchess.

Although she was now growing old, she was always amusing.

When he thought of her, he knew that she typified what he really desired in à women, but could not find.

As the Duchess of Manchester, she had stunned London with her beauty.

She had a kind of aura of innocence and purity about her which the Marquis remembered his father saying was most attractive.

Later, when after the death of her husband she became enamoured of the Marquess of Hartington, her behaviour was exemplary.

She never addressed him in public except coolly and by his title.

For many years even the most knowledgeable gossips were never quite certain if the Marquess was or was not her lover.

Even when eventually she married him and became the Duchess of Devonshire, she still had a dignity about her.

It made her outstanding, and no husband could have

asked for a more attentive wife.

"Why cannot more women be like that?" the Marquis asked himself as he buttoned his shirt.

In his own experience he found that women always wanted to flaunt the fact that he was theirs.

Only a week ago he had said to the present recipient of his affections:

"Do not look so pleased to see me when I come into a room where our friends are congregated."

"But I am pleased to see you, Osmond!" she had answered. "The moment you appear my heart leaps and I want to run into your arms!"

The Marquis retorted irritably that it was just the sort of thing he disliked because it led to people gossiping about him.

He had no desire for the husband of the lady in question to call him out in a duel.

Duels were firmly forbidden by Queen Victoria, but they still occasionally took place.

However the Marquis did not wish to be involved in one, especially when the "woman in the case", as far as he was concerned, was very dispensable.

"That is the whole trouble," he thought.

All the women with whom he had had affairs meant very little to him once he had had them in his arms.

He would have enjoyed scaling the heights of Abraham or diving down deep into the sea to capture them.

But he had only to take one step in their direction and their lips were turned up to his.

"Dammit all! What am I complaining about?" he asked his reflection in the mirror as he put the finishing touch to his evening-tie.

He shrugged himself into his exceedingly well-cut long-tailed coat.

Then he turned to look at Lady Sybil who was lying in a deliberately abandoned position on the crumpled bed.

"Thank you, Sybil," he said in his deep voice, "for a very enjoyable evening."

When she realised he was really going, she sat up revealing her exquisitely curved breasts.

"How can you be so cruel as to go when I want you to stay?" she asked.

The Marquis took her outstretched hand and lifted it perfuntcorily to his lips as he said:

"Go to sleep, Sybil. I shall expect you to look the most beautiful person at Devonshire House tomorrow."

Her fingers tightened on his.

"And we will be together again tomorrow night," she said softly. "Oh, Osmond, I love you so! I feel tomorrow will never come!"

He smiled at her, took his hand with some difficulty from hers and left the room quickly.

As she heard his footsteps going down the passage towards the stairs, she got out of bed wondering if she had been foolish to let him go.

However she resisted an impulse to run after him to prevent him from leaving.

"I will keep him with me longer tomorrow night!" she promised herself.

As the Marquis went down the stairs into the hall, a footman who was half-asleep rose quickly from the chair in which he had been sitting to open the front door.

The Marquis told himself he must think of a convincing excuse for not entering the house again.

It was impossible simply simply to tell a woman he was bored.

Usually he timed the ending of his love-affairs to coincide with a pressing engagement out of London, like the races at Newmarket, or the opening of the Shooting Season in Scotland.

Although at the moment he could find no good excuse

for not dining with Lady Sybil, he told himself confidently that he would think of one by the morning.

The night air was cold and sharp but as Westoak House was only a short distance from his own he had not ordered a carriage to wait for him.

Instead he walked, having a sudden vision of snow-capped mountains, or the waves of the sea storm-tossed in the Bay of Biscay.

'I have to stay in England for the moment,' he told himself.

Then he realised that the frost in the air had swept away the cloying heat and over-scented atmosphere of Sybil's bedroom.

By the time he reached Vale House he was feeling quite cold but invigorated.

He instructed the night-footman that he would ride in the morning at eight o'clock before breakfast.

Then he hurried up the stairs to his bedroom where his valet was waiting for him.

He undressed, saying as little as possible, as he was not conversational at this hour of the morning.

When he got into bed he did not immediately fall asleep, as he expected to do.

He found himself wondering once again why women so quickly palled on him.

He knew that his contemporaries would not believe it possible that he had no wish to touch Sybil again.

She was recognised to be one of the most beautiful women in London.

There seemed to be almost a profusion of such beauties.

All of them were to be found at Marlborough House, for the Prince of Wales, although he was growing older, had the same *penchant* for a pretty face that he had had since he was a very young man.

He certainly enjoyed the delights of love wherever he found them.

The Marquis saw no reason why he should not follow His Royal Highness's example.

It was not only that he was resisting marriage, despite the pleas of his relatives that he should produce an heir.

But he was also unusually fastidious in that he never took a mistress of a lower class than his own.

There was certainly no need for him to pay for his pleasures.

Also he thought the idea of keeping a discreet little house in St. John's Wood, as did most members of his Club, was somehow degrading.

Why should he want anything other than the well-bred Ladies of Quality.

They were, as he well knew, all anxious for his attentions and made it very obvious that they were interested in him the moment they saw him.

He turned over restlessly in his bed, saying as he did so:

'I am bored! Bored! Bored! Bored!'

His words seemed to echo in his ears until finally he fell asleep.

The next morning the Marquis found there had not only been a heavy frost in the night, but there was also a bitter wind blowing through the trees in Hyde Park.

There were few riders besides himself.

As he enjoyed the exercise he found the sharpness of the wind pleasingly invigorating.

However he realised he was hungry when he returned home for breakfast at nine o'clock.

There was the usual sideboard in the Dining-Room laden with silver entrée dishes filled with food to tempt him.

On the table there was a large pat of golden butter from his Jersey cows at Vale Park in Hertfordshire, and a pot of honey from his own bees.

Besides this there were hot scones, a small cottage-loaf

of fresh bread which his Chef had risen while it was still dark, to bake for him.

The Marquis however, was a careful eater as he had no desire to increase his weight.

He had no wish by the time he was the same age as the Prince of Wales, to look like him. He therefore took a great deal of exercise.

When he was in the country he rode round his estate in all weathers, only using a carriage if he was going out to dinner.

In consequence he had not a surplus ounce of flesh on his body.

As he rose from the breakfast table he was aware that there were half-a-dozen dishes still left untouched.

He knew that few other men in his position would notice it or think it a waste of food.

In fact, he supposed most of it would be finished in the Servants' Hall.

He had often on his travels had to exist for long intervals on very short rations, he therefore appreciated the value of what he ate.

He thought however as he left the Dining-Room that any criticism he might make would only upset and surprise the household.

They carried on in exactly the same way as they had when his father was alive.

Doubtless, too, there had been few changes since his grandfather's time.

He went to his Study where his Secretary, Mr. Bowes, had left his letters waiting for him on his desk.

Those that obviously concerned business or engagements had been opened.

However, those that were faintly scented or written with a flowing hand were put in a separate pile untouched.

The Marquis settled himself to open and read those

which were concerned with business.

The door opened and the Butler said:

"His Excellency the Ambassador of Siam, M'Lord!"

The Marquis looked up in surprise.

He had met the Siamese Ambassador several times before at parties, but could think of no reason why he should be calling on him at such an early hour.

He was a small man with hair that was just turning grey.

He bowed respectfully to the Marquis who rose from his desk to greet him.

Then he said in excellent English:

"You must forgive me, My Lord, for calling upon you so early, but I have urgent news from Bangkok which I felt should be conveyed to you without delay."

"Do sit down, Your Excellency," the Marquis invited, wondering as he spoke what the news could be.

The Ambassador seated himself on an upright chair and as the Marquis sat down near him he said:

"I am instructed by His Majesty King Chulalongkorn to inform you that Mr. Calvin Brook is dead!"

The Marquis started.

"Dead? Are you sure?"

"I was afraid, My Lord, you would find it somewhat of a shock, but the message from His Majesty informed me that you were to be the first to be told of Mr. Brook's decease."

He paused for a moment to let the news sink in before he continued:

"Moreover, if it is at all possible His Majesty would be exceedingly grateful if you could visit him in Bangkok immediately."

The Marquis stared at the Ambassador in astonishment.

He was extremely perturbed to hear of his friend's death, and it seemed very strange that King Chulalongkorn should wish to see him personally.

Then as he considered what he had been told, he knew the answer.

There was probably something strange about Calvin Brook's death.

More than that, something which undoubtedly involved diplomatic, and perhaps even more important problems.

The Marquis had met Calvin Brook several years ago in India.

He had been told then that he was a very strange and unusual man.

He guessed, although no one had said as much, that he was deeply involved in what was known as 'The Great Game.'

This was counter-espionage sevice to monitor Russian ambitions to conquer India by causing as much disturbance as possible amongst the tribesmen on the Frontier.

Then later he had met Calvin Brook unexpectedly in Nepal.

He found he was a man who was continually involved in a thousand different ways in National Politics, not only concerning India, but many other countries in the East.

He then had travelled widely with Calvin Brook.

Looking back, he thought it was a time of more excitement than he had ever known before or since in his life.

It was not only perils of sea, jungle or desert which confronted them.

He found himself helping to quell riots, anticipate uprisings, and a half-a-dozen times at least nearly forfeiting his life in the attempt.

It was an experience he would never forget.

He only left Calvin Brook when he had been forced to return home on his father's death.

Now he knew that Calvin was dead and it would be a greivous loss to the world.

On his return to England he had learnt from the Secretary for Foreign Affairs that Calvin Brook had been offered a peerage and various other distinctions.

He had refused them all.

It was typical of the man that he preferred to remain anonymous.

He had no wish to be beholden to anyone or indeed to belong to any particular country.

He just wished to be 'in the thick of things', and managed to turn up wherever there was a trouble-spot and by some miraculous means of his own, to take the heat out of it.

All this flashed through the Marquis's mind before he said:

"It cannot be true! It is impossible to believe that Brook is dead!"

"I think in fact, there is some mystery about it," the Ambassador said quietly, "and that is why His Majesty is asking for you."

Because the Marquis knew the Eastern mind so well, he was certain the Ambassador was being perceptive and finding more in the message he had received than was actually written down in words.

There was a long pause before the Marquis said:

"I will leave for Bangkok immediately! Will you telegraph His Majesty to expect me?"

The Ambassador's smile seemed to stretch from ear to ear.

"That is very gracious of Your Lordship, and I know how delighted His Majesty will be to receive you."

Then as the Marquis would have risen he added:

"There is one thing more. It would be very gracious of you, My Lord, since you knew Calvin Brook so well, if you will break the news of his death to his daughter."

The Marquis stared.

"I had forgotten he had a daughter!"

"She is in London at the moment under the chaperonage of her aunt, Lady Brook, the widow of Calvin Brook's brother."

"Of course I will call on her," the Marquis said.

"That is very kind of you," the Ambassador replied.

"I am afraid she will be very distressed by the loss of her father."

The Marquis was sure that was true.

He remembered that Calvin Brook had once told him that his wife had been dead for some years, and their only child, a daughter, was at the moment in Cairo.

"I left her there six months ago when I came East," he said. "She is with friends who will take her back to England where she will go to School."

He sighed before he went on:

"She has been travelling with me, but it is now essential she should be properly educated. But I miss her, I miss her very much!"

The Marquis had hardly listened and had in fact, thought that Calvin Brook would find his companionship a good deal more satisfactory than that of a child.

He now remembered Calvin Brook's concern before they had set out on their last expedition together, which had involved travelling in great discomfort through Burma and into Siam.

Calvin Brook had asked him then if anything happened to him whether he would undertake to be the Guardian of his daughter.

"I will do anything you like," the Marquis had said lightly, "but, for God's sake, take care of yourself!"

He had paused a moment before he went on:

"You are too valuable to be killed by a poisoned dart, or die of some jungle fever where there is no doctor within a hundred miles of us!"

Calvin Brook had laughed.

"I will try to do neither of those things! In fact where we are going we are far more likely to have a knife thrust in our back, or a bullet between our eyes, and have not the least idea who our assailant may be."

"I am glad you warned me!" the Marquis laughed.

He remembered that before they left to encounter the

dangers which Calvin Brook had described, he had sent a letter to England.

He had informed his Solicitors that in the event of his death, Lord Osmond Skelton-Vale would become the Guardian of his daughter Ankana.

"Yes, that is her name!" the Marquis said aloud. "Ankana!"

"In Siamese that means 'Beautiful Woman'," the Ambassador explained.

"Then let us hope she lives up to her name," the Marquis answered.

Soon after his conversation with the Ambassador of Siam the Marquis left to drive towards Belgravia where he learnt Miss Ankana Brook was staying with her aunt.

He wondered if she would in any way resemble her father who had been a good-looking man.

Or if she would be shy, gauche, and rather clumsy, as he thought young English girls were when he compared them to those of other nations.

He had been entranced by the grace and beauty of the Indian women.

The children with their huge dark eyes were like something out of a picture-book.

He could say the same about the girls in Ceylon.

He remembered thinking that the women of Bali and those of Siam had a grace that could not be found in the West.

"Too large, too heavy and too hearty!" he said to himself as his footman rang the bell of the house he was visiting.

Having asked for Miss Ankana Brook, he was shown into a well-furnished, but rather dull Drawing-Room.

He was sure it was identical with every other Drawing-Room in the whole Square.

As he waited he thought that Calvin would certainly not fit in with such conventionality.

He could see him wearing a *sarong* when it was hot, and nothing else.

He would walk up to his waist in the muddy water through which they had to travel in parts of the Malayan jungle.

As the door opened he turned to look in surprise at the girl who had just come in.

She was small by English standards, not more than five foot five, and she was very slim.

Her hair was dark and her eyes seemed enormous in a small heart-shaped face.

She was so different from what the Marquis had expected that he could only stare at her.

Then as she moved towards him he saw some resemblance to her father, but it was only vague and related more to his personality than his physical appearance.

"I was told you wanted to see me," she said. "Did Papa send you?"

She held out her hand as she spoke and as the Marquis took it he thought it seemed very small in his.

Yet there was something alive about it.

Just as he had felt if ever he touched Calvin Brook; that he radiated a vitality which he had never met in anyone else.

"Shall we sit down, Miss Brook?" the Marquis suggested gently.

"My name is Ankana," she replied, "and as I know Papa has asked you to be my Guardian if anything should happen to him, I think it seems absurd for you to address me in such a formal fashion."

"I agree with you," the Marquis said, "and you must forgive me if I ask you how old you are. I have, to be honest, not thought about you for some years."

"I am eighteen," Ankana replied.

The Marquis knew he had expected her to be several years younger than that.

She sat down on the sofa and as he lowered himself beside her she looked at him enquiringly, and he found it difficult to choose his words.

"I am afraid, Ankana, I have some distressing news for you."

She was very still, but she did not speak, and he went on:

"I have just been informed an hour ago by the Ambassador of Siam that he has received a message from His Majesty the King to say that your father is dead."

He knew even as he spoke that he was putting it abruptly and almost brutally.

He could not think how he could mitigate such upsetting news in a way that would make it easier to receive.

Ankana did not speak for a moment, then she said:

"That is not true! Papa is not dead!"

The Marquis stared at her.

"Why should you say that?"

"Because I know he is alive," she said. "He may be in a great deal of trouble, but he is not dead, whatever the King may say!"

For a moment the Marquis could not find words to answer and she asked:

"What are you going to do about it?"

"His Majesty has asked me to go out to Bangkok immediately. In fact I think there is some mystery about your father's death."

"That I can believe!" Ankana said. "But I know I would have been aware of it if he had died."

She paused a moment before she went on emphatically:

"I am completely and absolutely certain, although of course you may not believe me, that they cannot produce evidence to substantiate his death."

"I cannot understand how you can be so certain of this," the Marquis said. "I am sure the King of Siam, who is a very intelligent man, would not have sent such a message unless he had actual proof that your father is in fact dead."

"If anything had happened to Papa I would have known," Ankana said quietly. "When are you leaving for Bangkok?"

"I am going by train to Folkestone this afternoon, where I shall board my yacht, and if we are fortunate and the sea is not too rough, I shall be in Bangkok in a month's time."

"Then I will come with you!"

"That is impossible!" the Marquis retorted quickly.

"Why?"

"For one thing, you obviously cannot travel with me alone, and I have no intention of having a party."

He stopped speaking to look at her before he continued:

"Secondly, when I reach Bangkok I may have to go up country to look for your father, and if, as you suspect, he is alive, then he is more than likely to be in a position of some danger."

"In other words you think he is a prisoner!" Ankana said. "Personally, I think it more likely that he is in hiding."

"Why, and from whom?"

She made a little gesture with her hands that was very eloquent and very un-English.

"You have met Papa, you have travelled with him," she said, "and he is always unpredictable."

"That is certainly true," the Marquis agreed. "At the same time you have to face the truth, and it is true that your father takes more risks than most men."

"Which he enjoys tremendously," Ankana said, "and of course he has amazingly good luck! Or rather, as I know he would admit, he has special protection."

"From whom?" the Marquis could not stop himself from asking.

"From the Power in which he believed and which he has always used. He thinks of it as the 'Life Force', but in this country you would describe it rather conventionally as God!"

She spoke with a slightly scathing note in her voice which

made the Marquis look at her questioningly.

He found it difficult to understand her, and how she could be so positive that her father was alive.

As if she could read his thoughts she gave a little laugh and said:

"Papa and I have always been so close that we think in exactly the same way."

She smiled at him then went on:

"We have an affinity which they understand in the East, but which is quite incomprehensible to those who live in the West and accept nothing which cannot be set out on paper."

Now there was a definitely mocking note in her voice and the Marquis replied defensively:

"You can hardly expect me to believe something you cannot substantiate."

"When you find Papa alive, as you will, then there will be no argument about it," Ankana said. "I think, My Lord, if I am to accompany you, I had better go and get ready."

She got up as she spoke and the Marquis rose to his feet.

"Let me make it quite clear, Ankana," he said, "that I am not taking you with me. You are to stay here with your aunt, as your father arranged, and complete your education."

Ankana laughed.

"I left School, if that is what you mean by 'completing my education' before Christmas. What I am doing now is preparing to be presented to the Social World as a well-behaved, conventional débutante!"

She looked at him and gave a faint smile.

"But Papa needs me, and so thank goodness, I can forget all that nonsense!"

The Marquis sighed.

"I am afraid Ankana, that whatever you may sound to yourself you are very unconvincing to me. I have been told on first-class authority that your father is dead, and until I can prove otherwise I must accept what I have been told."

He knew from the way Ankana was looking at him that she thought he was being very stupid and it made him angry.

"I am going to Bangkok," he went on, "and if I find your father I will of course telegraph the Embassy immediately to inform you that he is alive."

He gave a deep sigh, and then continued:

"If not, I will find out everything I can about the circumstances of his death, and I will relate them to you in detail on my return."

He spoke as if to a recalcitrant child, and after a short silence Ankana said in a quiet voice:

"You will go to Bangkok as quickly as possible?"

"Of course," the Marquis replied. "My yacht, which is called '*The Sea Horse*', is, I promise you, faster than any other yacht of its kind afloat, and the new engines, which I have just had installed will take me to Siam as quickly as, if not faster than, an ocean liner."

"You will go aboard tonight?" Ankana asked.

"I shall leave within two hours at the outside for Folkestone."

He paused and then continued sternly:

"As my instructions to my Captain are always to have the yacht ready to sail at a moment's notice, we will be on our way before it is dark!"

"And when you see Papa will you tell him I am thinking of him and of course loving him?"

"I will give him your message," the Marquis promised in a gentler voice than he had used before. "I hope with all my heart, Ankana, that you are right and your father is alive, but I think it will be a mistake to be too optimistic."

"Papa always says one must look for the truth," Ankana said, "and although you may not believe me, that is what I am doing."

She held out her hand as she spoke and added:

"Thank you very much for going so quickly to Bangkok as the King has requested you to do. As you know Papa so well, I have a feeling he may be able to reveal to you where he is and I am certain you will find him."

"Again I can only say that I hope you are right," the Marquis said.

Although even as he spoke he heard the doubtful note in his own voice.

Once again he held Ankana's hand in his.

He thought as he looked down at her that she was very different from what he had expected.

"*Bon Voyage!*" she said, then added in Siamese: "And may the gods protect you!"

The Marquis stopped.

"Do you speak Siamese?"

"A little," Ankana admitted. "Are you thinking that I might be useful if I came with you?"

"No, no, of course not!" the Marquis said quickly. "Any young woman would only be an encumbrance on such a journey."

He paused a moment to say sternly:

"As I have already told you, I have no intention of having a party or, to be honest, to be encumbered by you when I get there."

"You are very frank," Ankana said, "but all I am concerned with, My Lord, is that you hurry!"

She stopped to look at him, and her eyes were alight with fear, as she continued:

"I know Papa is alive, but I think he is in a situation – in fact I am sure of it – where he needs help and I hope that is what you will be able to provide."

She spoke so positively that the Marquis felt it was useless to go on arguing with her that her father was dead.

Instead he said:

"Goodbye Ankana, and when I return I will see, as I

should have done before that you are introduced to my relatives who have girls of your own age, and will be only too delighted to entertain you."

"That is very kind of you, My Lord," Ankana said, "and of course, I should be exceedingly grateful!"

Again there was that mocking note in her voice which he disliked and felt was somehow impertinent.

It was as if she was laughing at him for being very foolish.

As he drove away he told himself he might have expected Calvin Brook's daughter to be different.

But what he did not expect was that she was so different that to his annoyance she treated him as if he could not understand what she was trying to say to him.

The Marquis was well aware that in the East the natives of nearly all countries he had visited believed they could contact each other by the power of thought.

A man would know what had happened 300 miles away weeks, perhaps months, before the official news of a death could reach him.

But that was not to say that sometimes there would be mistakes.

He was certain in his mind that Ankana, born of Western parents, however unusual she might be, should not be encouraged in her belief that her father was alive.

It could be nothing more than wishful thinking.

"I shall soon find out if she is right or wrong when I reach Bangkok," he told himself.

As soon as he arrived back at Vale House he began making preparations for the voyage.

He gave instructions to his Secretary to send a very expensive basket of orchids to Lady Sybil, and express his regrets at not being able to dine with her.

It was then he suddenly realised that he had been saved from her tears and recriminations, which he would have been unable to avoid had he stayed in London.

"It is an ill wind that blows nobody any good!" he thought.

Stepping into his carriage, and looking very smart in his travelling-clothes, he set off for the station.

He knew that a private compartment had been engaged on the train and that his Valet had gone ahead with his luggage.

As the horses drove down Park Lane he had the feeling that he was setting off on an adventure.

Ordinarily he would have been depressed and deeply saddened by the thought of Calvin Brook's death.

But despite his conviction that it was all nonsense, he found himself remembering the lilt and positiveness in Ankana's voice when she said:

"Papa is not dead. He is alive!"

Chapter Two

The Marquis, as had been arranged, found a private coach reserved for him on the train, which was fortunately an Express, to Folkestone.

He had an excellent luncheon provided by his own Chef, drinking with it half a bottle of his own champagne.

He was therefore in a good mood when the train pulled into Folkestone Station shortly after four o'clock.

His servants travelled with him, as well as his secretary.

He was bowed into a carriage which was waiting to convey him to the docks and his secretary followed him in another vehicle.

The '*Sea Horse*' was looking magnificent, out-shining all the other sea-going vessels in the harbour.

The flag of the Royal Yacht Club was flying from the mast, and the Captain was waiting at the top of the gang-plank for the Marquis's arrival.

He had received the telegram which had been sent hastily to Folkestone as soon as the secretary knew what his master intended.

The Marquis was piped aboard, and he could see that the Captain and crew were excited by the prospect of a long voyage.

He had taken the precaution of bringing with him from London many cases of wine and a large quantity of food.

He told the Captain that he wished to put to sea immediately.

Then before he went onto the bridge he took him into the Saloon to say:

"Our actual destination, Captain, is Bangkok, but I have no wish for my movements to be known to the Press. So do not inform the crew where we are going until we have actually left harbour."

"I assure you, My Lord, your intentions in the past have always been kept confidential," the Captain replied. "I will of course obey your instructions."

He paused a moment before continuing:

"I will not inform even the First Mate where we are going until we are at sea."

"Thank you," the Marquis said. "I will join you on the bridge in a few minutes."

He went down below to make sure that certain improvements he had ordered to be made the last time he had been aboard had been carried out.

He had taken the yacht to Algiers on her maiden voyage.

He had been delighted with the speed at which she travelled and the comfort that he found on board.

There were however a few details that he wished to rectify, and certain alterations made in the sleeping arrangements.

These now, he saw with satisfaction, were completed.

His own cabin, he thought, look particularly attractive and was decorated principally in a shade of green which he thought was appropriate to the sea.

He had also had a number of bookcases constructed which supplemented those in the Saloon.

He had known when he travelled in other people's yachts how infuriating it was to be a long time without sight of land unless one had plenty to read.

He had therefore made sure that there were a number of books that he himself found interesting.

He had also arranged that new volumes were automatically sent to the '*Sea Horse*' at the same time as they went to his Libraries in London and in the country.

Having found everything in order, he went up onto the bridge.

Joining the Captain he had watched him take the yacht out of harbour.

Once they were sailing down the English Channel the Marquis thought with satisfaction that he had left England.

Whatever problems lay ahead, a number of his worries, notably Lady Sybil, were no longer with him.

He knew it was only due to his superb ability at organisation that he had managed to get away so quickly.

He had given instructions to his Secretary as to who was to be notified of his departure.

He had also told him to make sure that everything would run smoothly until his return.

As he felt the yacht moving through the water, its speed increasing until he knew they were doing over seven knots with every likelihood of being able to do more, he was very proud.

He had personally supervised every detail in the '*Sea Horse*' and he knew that his engines were outstanding.

There were also gadgets and new inventions that were not to be found in any other yacht, or ship for that matter.

Aloud he said to the Captain:

"I would like to break all records in reaching Bangkok. What is your estimate of how long it will take?"

The Captain, who was a Scot and thought carefully before he spoke, replied:

"As Your Lordship knows, the P. and O. Liners boast that they now reach India in seventeen days. I think we can improve on that."

He paused to qualify his optimism by adding:

"That is if we are fortunate and do not run into heavy seas and it will take about five or six days more to reach Bangkok."

"I have been hoping it will be under three weeks," the

Marquis said.

"Perhaps we may be able to surprise Your Lordship!" the Captain answered.

"I shall be extremely gratified if you do!" the Marquis replied.

When he went below, the Marquis changed for dinner in exactly the same way as he would have done if he had had a party aboard.

He enjoyed an excellent meal cooked by his French Chef and his assistant, who was Chinese.

The Marquis again went up on the bridge before he turned in.

There he found he had definitely underestimated the speed at which his yacht could travel.

There was a satisfied smile on his lips when he went down to the Master Cabin.

He found his valet had everything unpacked and ready for him.

"So far, so good! Dobson," he said, as the man helped him out of his evening-coat.

"It's a treat, My Lord, to be setting out on our own again, so to speak."

The Marquis smiled.

Dobson had attached himself to the Marquis when he had visited Singapore, but not then in the position of valet.

He had in fact been his 'general factotum', a 'Jack of all Trades'.

The Marquis had found him indispensable in the strange places he had visited alone and then later in the company of Calvin Brook.

He was well aware that like himself Dobson was bored with the well-organised social life they were living in England.

The moment the Marquis had said they were going abroad, Dobson's eyes had lit up.

He moved with the quickness of a kingfisher.

Now, knowing that Dobson was consumed with curiosity as to what was happening, the Marquis said:

"I expect you know that this morning the Ambassador of Siam called on me? He came to inform me that Mr. Brook is dead."

Dobson stared at him.

"Are you certain of that, M'Lord?"

"His Majesty the King of Siam telegraphed instructions to his Embassy to inform me of his death."

He stopped speaking to give emphasis to his words before he went on:

"He said he very much wanted to see me, and as the matter appeared to be urgent, I acceded to His Majesty's request."

"I wouldn't mind bettin', M'Lord, that Mr. Brook ain't any more dead than wot I am!"

"Why on earth should you say that?" the Marquis asked.

"If they'd got "is body on their 'ands," Dobson explained, "it stands to reason they'd ship it back to where he belongs."

This was something the Marquis had not thought of, and he thought it was astute of Dobson.

At the same time he told himself it was very unlikely that the King had been deceived into believing Calvin Brook was dead if in fact he was alive.

It would certainly be a mistake to raise anybody's hopes only to disappoint them.

Aloud he said:

"I am sure it is unlucky to speculate on what at the moment seems extremely improbable."

"Nothing's improbable where Mr. Brook's concerned," Dobson replied, 'an' if Your Lordship asks me, I reckon he's up to one of his 'monkey-tricks'!"

"I am not asking you!" the Marquis answered quickly. "And I intend to believe what I am told until it can be proved otherwise."

Dobson did not reply.

When he left the Cabin the Marquis thought irritably:

"First Ankana, now Dobson!"

The whole thing was ridiculous!

He was sure that if the King wanted to see him it was for some other reason than to prove that Calvin Brook was alive.

What he guessed was that Calvin Brook had been involved in some very delicate piece of espionage which had resulted in his death.

This was probably of such vital importance that the King was going to ask him to carry on where Calvin Brook had left off.

He knew as few others did the amazing successes they had had together in the past.

The Marquis was aware there was a file marked '*Top Secret*' in the Foreign Office which recorded his and Calvin Brook's exploits in India and in other parts of the East.

He had thought when he inherited his title that that part of his life was finished.

He could not however suppress a little flicker of excitement within himself at the thought that soon he might once again be travelling in disguise to some obscure part of Siam.

Or perhaps he would be travelling to Burma for a purpose known only to the King and his Senior Ministers.

When King Chulalongkorn had ascended the throne, he was only fifteen.

In the years that followed his accession he had in an astonishing degree revolutionised his Court and his country in a thousand different ways.

He had started immediately by ending the ancient custom of presentation.

He allowed officials to sit on chairs during their audiences.

This had been an incredible innovation in Siam.

Every King before him had been approached in a kneeling position with a humbly bowed head.

He had then abolished serfdom in sensible stages, giving owners and serfs time for readjustment.

Even more surprisingly he had replaced the age-old system of *corvee* labour by direct taxation.

The Marquis had understood that as King Chulalongkorn's reign continued it had constituted the most complete revolution proceeding from the throne which had ever taken place in the world.

Siam had previously had no Schools, roads, railways, hospitals, or even a properly equipped Army.

To achieve this enormous task of modernisation the King had brought in foreign advisers.

He sent his sons and other young men of the Court to European Capitals for their education.

In conformity with the King's policy, and as a token of friendship, the Tsar of Russia, Nicholas II, asked for one of the Royal Princes to be brought up by him in Russia.

The King accepted the offer.

He chose Prince Chakrabongse to go to St. Petersburg to attend the *Corps des Pages*, a Military Academy.

On being commissioned the Prince served in the Emperor's own Hussar Guards.

The Marquis, having met the King, had been extremely impressed by his alert brain.

They had become friends. In fact, it was largely due to him that the King during his European tour the previous year had visited England.

His Majesty had stayed at Buckingham Palace.

Queen Victoria was resting at Windsor in preparation for her Diamond Jubilee and he was received by the Prince of Wales.

The tour included Russia, Sweden and Belgium.

A prime factor in its great success was that the King was the first Asian Monarch who could talk to his hosts in English instead of through an interpreter.

When he returned home, he had written the Marquis a most charming letter.

He said how much he had enjoyed seeing him again, and how delightful he had found everything in England.

"Whatever he asks me to do," the Marquis thought now, "it will be very difficult to refuse him."

He also wanted to see the alterations the King had made in Bangkok since his last visit.

As he got into bed he was thinking with real enthusiasm of what lay ahead.

Only just before he fell asleep did he realise with a sense of relief that he was alone.

If he had not received that urgent message from the King he might have been unable to avoid Lady Sybil.

In which case he would have been bored to the point where he had no wish to see her again.

As he stretched out in his large, comfortable bed, he told himself that once again his luck had not failed him.

If there were reproaches and the inevitable tears from Lady Sybil, they would certainly not worry him now.

By the time he returned she would doubtless have found another lover to take his place.

The Marquis awoke to find the '*Sea Horse*' was pitching and tossing.

It did not worry him because he was an excellent sailor.

He only hoped that everything had been battened down competently and there would not be a lot of breakages.

He was quite certain the yacht itself was entirely sea-worthy.

It had been through every possible test both in the Ship-yard before it was launched and during its sea-trials.

The weather was very cold, but he had discovered and installed a new method of heating the cabins.

It was only when he went up on deck that he realised how

biting the wind was, and there were undoubtedly snow-clouds in the sky.

"The sooner we find the sunshine the better," he said to the Captain when he reached the bridge.

"We've not had to drop our speed so far, M'Lord," the Captain replied proudly.

The Marquis not only spent a long time on the bridge, but also inspected the seamen's quarters.

He found they were pleased with the comfortable way they had been designed.

Every man was exceedingly proud of the yacht and made it clear to the owner that they were delighted to be in his service.

The Marquis had always known that a happy ship was only possible if every man aboard was comfortably accommodated and properly fed.

He had made this absolutely clear to the Chef.

When he engaged him he said that he expected the best food available for himself and his guests.

He also expected his crew to have meals which would build up their health and strength and which they would also enjoy.

He had had a row with his last Chef when he had discovered there had not been enough fresh fruit and vegetables taken aboard at Gibraltar.

He was confident that such a situation would not arise again.

By the afternoon they were entering the Bay of Biscay.

The Marquis knew that this was when the real test of the '*Sea Horse*' would take place.

The seas in January were very different from those they would have encountered in June.

Far from being anxious or apprehensive, however, the Marquis was looking forward to the challenge.

He was delighted before he retired for the night to find

that the '*Sea Horse*' had 'held her own'.

This was despite a tempestuous sea and a very rough wind!

At the same time, it was wise to move about the yacht slowly and carefully.

It would be foolish to risk a broken leg while she was inevitably pitching and tossing.

When he went to bed, the sharpness of the wind and the strain of taking care in moving about the yacht had made him tired.

He fell asleep as soon as his head touched the pillow.

When the Marquis awoke he knew immediately that the worst of the storm was over.

There was sunshine coming through the port-holes and he guessed they were somewhere near Lisbon.

Because he was in a hurry, he had arranged that the first stop, unless there was any damage to the ship, would be Gibraltar.

When Dobson called him his first question was:

"Is everything all right?"

"Everythin', M'Lord. Nothin's smashed or damaged but a few plates in the galley," Dobson assured him, "and a wine-glass which Yer Lordship left in the Saloon and was overlooked."

The Marquis laughed.

He knew that Dobson liked to catch him out whenever it was possible.

He said with pretended severity:

"It was careless of the steward not to have seen it!"

"You put it down on the floor by the chair in which you was reading, M'Lord," Dobson said, "an' he's used to gentlemen as puts their glasses on the table."

The Marquis would never have let such impertinence go unrebuked from anyone but Dobson.

But Dobson had known him when he was unimportant

and they had been in some very dangerous situations together.

He therefore, allowed the man far more licence than anybody else in his employment.

It was later that day when the Marquis came down to change for dinner that Dobson said:

"The bolt on the cabin next to Your Lordship's must 'ave slipped into place when we was a-tossin' and turnin' last night."

He paused a moment before he went on:

"The Ship's Carpenter 'as tried to free it, but he says he can't do nothin' except force the lock, and that means makin' a mess o' the new paint."

"Then leave it alone!" the Marquis said sharply. "If it slipped into place during a storm, it will very likely slip back if we have another one. We are not using that cabin?"

"I'd put a few of Your Lordship's clothes in the wardrobe," Dobson replied, "but I can use the others."

"There are plenty of them," the Marquis said in an amused voice, "and if that is all you have got to complain about, I am very grateful."

He knew the Captain was as elated as he was.

The '*Sea Horse*' had come through magnificently what had been a very unpleasant storm.

From now on they would be moving into smoother waters and leaving the frost and cold behind them.

Again the Marquis had an excellent dinner.

Afterwards, just as he had the night before, he looked up some of the phrases he would find useful in Siam.

It was a very difficult language, he decided.

He could speak a certain amount of Urdu, and could make himself understood in Caylon.

But he had not really been in Siam long enough to pick up much of the language.

Yet because he was a perfectionist, he had every intention of trying.

As he started to translate "*Sangitiyavangs*" a history of Buddhist synods, he thought what he really needed was a teacher.

Although he doubted if he would be in the country long enough to employ one.

It was quite late when he went down below.

After Dobson had left him he was just about to get into bed when he realised he had left *Sangitiyavangs*" upstairs in the Saloon.

He put out his hand towards the bell, then thought he might as well fetch it himself.

He put on the warm robe which lay on the end of his bed.

Walking carefully along the passage because the yacht was still rolling, he climbed up the companionway and went into the Saloon.

His book was where he had left it.

When he had put it under his arm he stood for a moment looking out into the darkness.

The storm-clouds had now disappeared and the sky was brilliant with stars.

He wanted to go out on deck and look at them, but he knew it would be very cold.

As he was now undressed, he had no intention of risking getting a chill which could be extremely unpleasant if it affected the kidneys.

Instead with a little sigh, as if he was missing something he wanted to enjoy, he went down the companionway.

He walked along the passage towards his cabin which filled the whole of the stern and had port-holes on either side of it.

He had almost reached the door and had his hand outstretched on the wall to help keep his balance.

Then, as he passed the door which Dobson had told him was bolted, he heard the unmistakable sound of a sneeze.

For a moment he thought he must be imagining it.

He stopped and listened, holding onto the lintel for support, and heard a soft movement inside the cabin.

It was incredible, and yet because he questioned his own hearing he put his ear against the door.

Now there was no doubt that somebody was moving about inside.

It was then an extraordinary thought flashed through the Marquis's mind.

He could not believe he was not imagining such a thing.

Yet he knocked on the door, saying as he did so:

"Open this door at once I know you are inside and I expect you to obey me!"

He did not raise his voice as he had no wish to attract the attention of any of the crew.

Like Dobson, they would be at the other end of the yacht.

He was sure however that anybody inside the cabin would be able to hear him quite clearly.

For the moment there was silence.

Then the Marquis's hearing, which was very acute, told him that somebody was moving slowly, and he thought, reluctantly towards the door.

"Draw back the bolt," he ordered, "or I shall fetch the Ship's Carpenter!"

Again there was a little pause.

Then there was the sound of the bolt being pulled back, and the Marquis turned the handle.

He opened the door and saw, as he expected, Ankana was standing just inside.

There was a light in the cabin, but she had shaded it cleverly so that no light could be seen from outside.

As the Marquis entered the cabin he saw that pillows also had been placed along the bottom of the door.

A light showing beneath might have alerted somebody outside to the fact that it was occupied.

For the moment he was too angry to speak.

Then as she looked up at him, her eyes very large in her small face, he said:

"What are you doing here?"

It was an unnecessary question and he knew the answer before she said a little hesitatingly:

"I . . I am sorry . . but I had to come with you . . and find . . Papa."

"How dare you!" the Marquis thundered. "And how could you have come aboard undetected?"

There was a faint smile on her lips as she replied:

"There were a great number of tradesmen coming and going after your telegram arrived, and the seamen were all busy cleaning and polishing the ship."

"I told you that I could not take you with me!"

"I will not get in your way," Ankana said, "and there is plenty of room, as I found when I came below."

"That is not the point!" the Marquis snapped. "The only thing I can do now is to send you back from Gibraltar."

"In which case I will go to Bangkok overland!"

"You will do nothing of the sort!" the Marquis said angrily. "I am your Guardian, and you will obey me!"

To his surprise, instead of being frightened because he was raving at her, Ankana laughed.

"Do you really expect me to do everything you tell me?" she asked. "I am sure Papa would find that very funny."

"If you ask me, I think your father would be disgusted at your behaviour!" the Marquis snapped.

Ankana shook her head.

"No, he would not! When I ran away from School to be with him in Morocco, he merely laughed and said that I was a 'chip off the old block'!"

She paused a moment, and laughed again, before she went on:

"It was what he himself had done once when he was at Harrow."

"You are the most infuriating girl I have ever met!" the Marquis exclaimed.

What he said would have sounded more impressive if at that moment the ship had not lurched.

In order to prevent himself from falling he had had to sit down on the bed.

He was thinking as he did so that it would be extremely difficult when they got to Gibraltar to find somebody who would convey her back to London.

Then, as if she refused to go, he was not quite certain what he could do about it.

She must have read his thoughts because she said:

"However much you may try to prevent it, I intend to go to Bangkok. You must try to understand that I have to be with him!"

The Marquis took a deep breath.

"Now listen, Ankana," he said in a different tone of voice, "you have to be sensible about this. The King of Siam and a large number of other people believe that your father is dead."

He saw that Ankana was about to argue, and he went on:

"If, when we reach Bangkok, I am convinced that you are right and he is alive, I swear to you that I will do everything in my power to find him and, if he is in hiding, bring him back."

The Marquis looked at Ankana to see if she was listening and continued:

"If you are with me, you will only make things more difficult for me. How can I possibly explain how, even if you are your father's daughter, you are travelling alone with me?"

He paused a moment to smile at her before he went on:

"And where can I find a chaperon without wasting a great deal of time, when I should be on my way to Siam?"

"I have thought of that," Ankana said calmly.

She had sat down in an armchair that was battened to the

floor and looked, the Marquis thought, very much at her ease.

He realised she was wearing only a nightgown and over it a dressing-gown not elaborate enough to be called a *négligée*.

Its colour was Nile blue and it fastened at the neck with a little round collar edged with lace.

Her dark hair, which was very long, was falling over her shoulders.

As if she was telling him what to think, she said:

"You are thinking that I look very young and that of course is the answer! I can look even younger, and everybody will believe you if you say I am fourteen or fifteen."

She gave him a lovely smile before she went on:

"That would make it perfectly all right, as you are my Guardian, for me to accompany you, and your precious reputation will be quite safe!"

"It is not my reputation I am worried about!" the Marquis protested.

"Oh, yes, it is!" Ankana flashed. "You are not in the least concerned about mine. It is simply that you feel embarrassed at the thought of arriving in Siam on what is an urgent secret mission."

She stopped speaking and lowered her voice before she went on:

"And you might be seen bringing with you somebody to amuse you, who the Social World which matters so much to you will assume she is your mistress!"

The Marquis sat upright.

"How dare you speak to me in such a way!" he said angrily. "It is exceedingly impertinent, and certainly not the way any Lady should talk!"

Ankana groaned.

"I cannot bear it if you start fussing about my being a Lady!" she said. "I had nearly two years of it at School, and now you are as bad as Papa's sister, who keeps saying:

" 'A Lady does not do this,' or 'A Lady does not do that!' until I could scream!"

"As I imagine she is screaming at the moment!" the Marquis remarked. "What excuse did you give her for leaving London?"

"I told the truth," Ankana replied. "I left her a message to say that I was going to Bangkok with you, as Papa needed me."

The Marquis was speechless.

Then almost as if he could not help himself, he said:

"You must have left for Folkestone as soon as I went from your house!"

"Travelling with Papa, I learnt how to do these things very quickly," Ankana replied. "I packed what I needed and slipped out of the house before my aunt came downstairs."

She smiled before she went on:

"I only stopped at the Bank to draw out plenty of money in case, as you have already threatened, you threw me out at Gibraltar, and arrived in Folkestone, nearly two hours before there was any sign of you!"

"I consider you have behaved extremely badly!" the Marquis said coldly.

"Of course I have, from your point of view! It would have been much easier if you had been pleasant and understanding, which of course was too much to expect, and had agreed to take me in the first place!"

He tried in vain to think of some way of getting rid of her which could preclude her travelling to Bangkok alone.

He was uncomfortably sure that she would, if necessary do her utmost to fulfil that threat.

"You might as well make the best of a bad job," Ankana said as he did not speak. "I promise I will not get in your way any more than is unavoidable, and when we reach Bangkok, I will find Papa."

"I thought that was what I was supposed to do," the

Marquis could not resist saying.

"I doubt if you will be very successful," Ankana said. "You are far too English, far too prosaic, and far too 'stuck in the mud' to be of any use in a situation like this."

The Marquis was again speechless.

Then as if she thought she had gone too far, Ankana said:

"Please . . I am not being rude . . I am only telling you what is the truth, and I have found all the Englishmen I have met are the same."

She hesitated before continuing:

"They only believe what they can see . . touch . . and have no . . conception at all of what the Chinese call so intelligently 'The World Behind the World'."

The Marquis believed himself to be perceptive and intelligent, but he was too stunned into silence to say so.

He had grown so used in the last two years to women fawning on him and flattering him.

So he had actually begun to take such adulation for granted, apart from the fact that he had a high estimation of himself.

"I suppose," Ankana went on, "if we are to work together, which is essential if we are to help Papa, we must in the first place, be frank with each other."

"I thought that was what you were just being!" the Marquis said wryly. "Or is there worse to come?"

She gave a little laugh which told him that she was pleased he was not sulking at what she had said.

"You may think it a great deal worse," she said, "but I hope not. I want to trust you. I know that Papa liked you."

The Marquis inclined his head at the concession, but she continued:

"I have however, heard about you from my aunt and a great number of other people, and it has made me suspicious and of course, wary."

"What have you heard?" the Marquis asked.

He thought it was rather *infra dig* to be curious, and yet

he could not help himself.

"First, they have gone into eulogies over you!" Ankana said. "Aunt Alice had of course heard about your friendship with Papa."

She smiled at him before she went on:

"She was always trying to make me write to tell you that I was in London, hoping you would ask me, and of course her, to dinner."

"I would have done so," the Marquis replied.

" . . very reluctantly!" Ankana finished. "When I heard what a success you were with the beautiful ladies who think you are a gift from Heaven to women, I knew we would have very little in common."

"If you talk to me like that," the Marquis said, "I think I shall give you a good spanking, as your father should have done years ago, if he had done his duty!"

Ankana laughed and the sound seemed to ring round the cabin.

"I am sure if Papa knew you were wasting your brain, your energy, and your time with a lot of empty-headed foolish women, whose only contribution to the world is to have their faces on picture post-cards in shop-windows, he would have said you were being a fool!"

"I have made a number of speeches in the House of Lords," the Marquis said defensively.

He paused to give authority to his words.

"Apart from running my estates I am also actively concerned with several National Charities which everybody in England thinks are vitally needed at the moment."

He wondered as he spoke why he should condescend to try to justify himself to this impertinent young woman.

Ankana's answer was one he did not expect.

"Of course in your position those are all the right things for you to do."

She smiled at him before she went on:

"I was only explaining why there is no place for me in

your life at this moment, and anyway, seeing the type of lady you like, we should have nothing in common except our love for Papa."

"Which is, of course, the most important!" the Marquis said.

He decided the best thing he could do was to ignore her innuendoes about his lady-friends.

Those he thought, if he chose to admit them, were not unjustified.

"On that we are agreed," Ankana said. "So now, if you are prepared to listen, shall I point out to you the simplest way I can travel with you?"

She tilted her head on one side, as she asked the question, before she said:

"I could be a young School-girl who, as Papa's daughter, you are very kindly being my Guardian, and bringing me with you."

"I suppose that is as good an explanation as any other for your presence," the Marquis said, "and I hope you can look young enough to be convincing."

"I would not be Papa's daughter, if I could not act a part," Ankana said proudly. "When we were in Africa, I was a Bedouin wife, and nobody suspected I was anything else."

She sighed as if with pleasure and added:

"When we were in the Sudan I was his son! All the Sheiks were completely deceived and allowed me to ride their horses astride without having the least idea I ought to be shut away in a Harem!"

The Marquis laughed as if he could not help it. Then he said:

"I suppose I shall have to accept your suggestion, but when we get to Bangkok you will do what I tell you."

His voice deepened as he went on:

"You will not run into any danger, even if I have to lock you in this cabin to prevent it!"

"Woof, woof!" Ankana smiled. "Now you are trying to frighten me! But as I know you are far too much of a gentleman to hurt me in any way, I am not impressed!"

"You may well find that I am quite different from what you imagine!" the Marquis replied ominously.

Ankana laughed.

"At least you will have somebody to bully, and argue with," she said. "From what Aunt Alice has told me, I gather that you sit like a Pasha while women reverently kiss your feet and tell you you are wonderful!"

"If I hear any more of what your aunt or anybody else has said about me," the Marquis observed, "I shall put you in a packing-case and send you back to England by train!"

"That is a new idea!" Ankana exclaimed. "I wonder if one could survive such a journey?"

She gave a little laugh, before she added:

"It is an interesting thought, and far easier than taking prisoners in chains or sending them for trial handcuffed to a prison-officer!"

The Marquis realised that any threat he might make would be thrust aside deftly.

She would listen only to what she wanted to hear.

He rose from the bed and holding onto the bedpost said:

"We shall have plenty of time to discuss our strategy, if we have one, when we reach Bangkok. Now I intend to go to bed, and I expect you will be quite capable of making explanations to my Valet for your presence here in the morning."

"Of course!" Ankana murmured.

"As for the Captain," the Marquis went on, "he will doubtless reproach himself bitterly for having allowed you to come aboard without anyone's knowledge!"

"In other words, I have caused a commotion which they will find very regrettable," Ankana said. "But do not worry, because like all men they enjoy surprises, and will soon grow used to me."

The Marquis did not relish the idea that men might accept her while a woman would not.

Yet he did not wish to labour the point at this moment.

He merely walked towards the door.

Only as he reached it did Ankana say:

"Goodnight, My Lord, and thank you for not throwing me overboard and feeding me to the fishes!"

"That is certainly an idea," the Marquis replied, "if you annoy me beyond endurance!"

He did not wait for her reply.

But he heard her laugh as he shut the door, and thought she was incorrigible.

Only when he was in bed did he think to himself that although he was extremely annoyed at Ankana sneaking aboard in such an irresponsible fashion, he might find her slightly amusing.

At least she would be somebody to talk to on what he knew however fast the yacht steamed, would be a long voyage.

Chapter Three

As the yacht moved down the Mediterranean the Marquis had to admit that Ankana was no trouble.

They had luncheon and dinner together.

The rest of the time she was either in her cabin or else in some sheltered place on deck where she was out of the wind.

He knew she was reading.

Only when they had sailed for some way that he became aware that the volumes on which she was concentrating were written in Siamese.

Half-jokingly he said at luncheon:

"I suppose, as you are so much better at Siamese than I am, I ought to ask you to teach me."

She looked at him in an enigmatic way, as if she was looking deep into him to see if he told the truth.

Then she said a little reluctantly:

"I do not think, considering what you . . feel about me, that you would be a . . good pupil."

"How do you know what I feel about you?" the Marquis said.

He knew it was a question to which he would be given a candid answer.

"Irritating, unpredictable and a nuisance!" Ankana said without pausing, and he laughed.

"I expected you to have a higher opinion of yourself than that."

"I have," she answered, "but I know that is what you are thinking, and in such circumstances, we have not the rapport which I assure you is traditionally important between a pupil and a teacher!"

As this was undoubtedly true, the Marquis thought it would be a mistake to argue.

Instead he said:

"I deliberately have not asked you before, but now I would like you to explain to me exactly why you are so certain that your father is still alive."

He had been watching her for the last three days.

He had known, because she was obviously passionately fond of her father, that she could not have seemed so much at ease and at times happy, unless she were convinced he was not dead.

Luncheon was finished and the servants had left them with only the coffee on the table.

The Marquis had in front of him a small glass of port.

The sun was shining through the windows of the Saloon and the sky seemed as blue as the Mediterranean itself.

In the distance the snow-capped summits of the mountains of Crete looked very lovely.

With its grey barrow rocks and touches of red on its cliffs the Marquis had stood for a long time thinking how beautiful it all looked.

He had always felt himself moved by snow-clad mountain peaks.

He told himself however important he might find his work in England, one day he would return to the Himalayas.

Now, as he realised that Ankana was looking at the mountains as if for inspiration, he said unexpectedly:

"Why do you hesitate to answer me?"

"I am asking myself," Ankana replied after a moment's pause, "whether you will understand if I tell you the truth, and also if it is wise for you to know too much."

The Marquis was astounded.

"What do you mean by that?"

She turned her head slowly to look at him.

"I suppose you know," he said, "that I find it infuriating when somebody will not answer a simple question!"

"It may seem simple to you," Ankana replied, "but in that case, you are only skimming over the surface, and not trying to understand the depths beneath which are far more important than words."

Because the Marquis was curious, he said in a voice that most women found irresistible:

"I can only beg you to trust me."

Ankana gave a little sigh, then she said:

"Very well, I will explain quite simply what I have already told you but you did not believe me."

She paused a moment and then added with emphasis:

"Papa and I are so linked together by our thoughts that, if he is dead, as you have been told he is, I would not be able to get in touch with him."

"Are you telling me that you can get in touch with your father, now, at this moment?" the Marquis asked, and his voice was incredulous.

"I would not try to do so while I am sitting here with you," Ankana replied, "but last night I tried to reach him and was reassured that he is alive and thinking of me."

She spoke so simply that it was hard for the Marquis not to believe her.

Although his common sense told him that what she was saying was impossible and that it was merely a part of her imagination.

"Perhaps I could make it a little clearer to you," Ankana said as he did not speak, "when I tell you that when I was a child Papa taught me to hear and obey him when we were some distance from each other."

She glanced at the Marquis to see if he understood.

When she was sure he did not, she explained more simply:

"I used to hide from my Nanny, then when a little older from my Governess, in the wood surrounding our house in the country, and when they were unable to find me, they would go to Papa and say:

" 'If you please, Sir, would you be kind enough to call Miss Ankana? I've no idea where she can be!' "

"And what did your father do?" the Marquis asked.

"He would send out his thoughts to me, and when I received them I knew I had to obey him, even though I did not wish to return to the house."

"How old were you when you did this?"

"I think it started when I was four or five," Ankana replied, "and after that, we were so attuned to each other, as you would say, that he would know when I needed him."

She stopped speaking and smiled at him before she added:

"In the same way, he would get in touch with me, wherever I might be."

"I find it hard to believe," the Marquis said, "but shall I tell you that I accept what you have told me? Now Ankana, I would like you to tell me, if you are aware of it, what your father is doing now."

Ankana's eyes were back on the snowy tops of the mountains and he knew she was concentrating on her father.

She was absolutely still, seeming hardly to breathe.

He thought that he had noticed almost subconsciously that there was a serenity about her that he had not found in any other woman.

He had been continually annoyed by women who fidgeted.

Sybil for instance had a habit of twiddling the rings on her fingers round and round.

"Why do you not keep still?" he had asked her once, and

she replied, as he might have expected:

"Because my fingers, darling, are itching to touch you, and I am restless because I am not in your arms!"

The Marquis remembered another great beauty who had begun to bore him, simply because she was eternally fiddling with her hair, patting and smoothing it.

He was not certain whether she was really worried in case it was untidy.

He suspected she merely wished to show off the shapely lines of her very lovely arms.

They must have sat for several minutes more before Ankana said:

"I am certain that Papa is in disguise . . I cannot for the moment see what it consists of . . but he is not himself!"

She sat in silence again before she went on:

"He is also in danger . . but at the moment he has control over it . . and while it is all round him . . his life is not immediately threatened."

She gave a deep sigh as if she had been holding her breath.

When she turned her head towards the Marquis, he had a feeling she was not really seeing him.

"How can you possibly know all this?" he asked after a moment. "And does it really help us?"

"I think perhaps it will be easier when we are nearer Papa," Ankana replied.

She got up from the table and crossed the cabin to kneel on the sofa and look out through the window.

When the Marquis had designed the Saloon he had refused to have any port-holes on one side of it.

Instead there were very large plate-glass windows which had been reinforced with steel so that they were extremely strong.

It gave an uninterrupted view of whatever they were passing as no port-hole could possibly have done.

Now, sitting at the table, the Marquis could see

Ankana's profile as she gazed out to sea.

Her long dark hair which had blue lights in it flowed nearly to her waist.

He was aware almost as if it was a surprise that she was very lovely.

The day after the Marquis had discovered Ankana hiding in the cabin she appeared early in the morning wearing a pretty gown.

It took him a moment or two to realise that she had shortened it by turning up the hem.

Her hair was left loose as would be correct in a girl of fourteen.

She had a ribbon round it which was tied in a small bow on top of her middle parting.

She was very slender, in fact, the Marquis thought, far too thin for her age.

She therefore looked exactly what she purported to be: a young girl not yet come to maturity.

Looking at her now the Marquis thought, though he had not at first been aware of it, she was in fact, unusually pretty.

Perhaps he substituted, 'beautiful' was the right word, in a manner that was so different from the women who were admired in London.

Her eyes were very expressive with their long, dark, eye-lashes which curled back like a child's.

They dominated her face, giving her what he could only describe to himself as a 'spiritual look', and that again was unexpected.

When however she was teasing him or arguing fiercely as they found themselves doing at almost every meal, there would be a glint in her eyes.

Also a mischievous curve to her lips which made her look very different.

"What are you thinking?" the Marquis asked sharply.

He thought that she was shutting him out from something which was important.

At first she did not answer. Then she said:

"Actually, I was praying to the gods who live on top of every mountain to look after Papa, which I am sure they will do."

"Why should you think the gods live on the tops of the mountains?" the Marquis asked.

"The gods, and spirits, have always come down when they visit mankind," Ankana replied. "I have never heard of one going up!"

The Marquis laughed.

"That is certainly true."

"They came down from Olympus, and the monks believe there were spirits or gods who lived on top of the Himalayas," Ankana said dreamily, "and therefore they will never be conquered."

"You have seen the Himalayas?" the Marquis asked in surprise.

"Papa and I once visited a monastery in the foothills," Ankana answered. "It was a long time ago, but I have never forgotten."

The Marquis, because the Himalayas meant something special to him, was interested.

He wanted to talk about it further, but as if it was something she felt was too sacred or important to her to discuss with him, Ankana said:

"Now that luncheon is finished, I expect you will want to be alone, so I will leave you."

He was just about to say there was no need for her to hurry away when she had gone.

He sat for a long time at the table thinking how strange she was.

How different from everything he expected to find in a young girl.

Later in the day he saw her when he was on the bridge watching the porpoises.

There were some half-a-dozen of them, swimming in the

wake of the yacht as if they were racing it.

Now and then they leapt out of the water in pairs.

Two days later they reached the Suez Canal.

Both the Marquis and Ankana were excited at seeing again de Lesseps silver link between the Mediterranean and the Red Sea.

The '*Sea Horse*' carried the flag of the Royal Yacht Club.

She therefore received the same privileges as the Royal Navy and did not have to pay harbour dues.

Moreover the Marquis's importance fortunately saved them from having to wait for a Pilot at Port Said.

Despite the fact that there was a number of much larger ships waiting, they went ahead without delay.

When they entered the Bitter Lakes it began to get really warm.

An awning was erected on the deck and the Marquis warned Ankana not to go into the sunshine without a hat or a sunshade.

"Perhaps I would be less trouble to you if I was confined to my bed!" she teased.

"On the contrary," he said, "I am quite resigned now to believing you are indispensable."

She smiled at him and asked provocatively:

"Are you being nice to me because you feel I may be useful?"

"That is one way of putting it," the Marquis said. "In any case we can hardly rant and roar at each other all the way to Bangkok!"

"It is you who were doing that, not me!" Ankana flashed.

The Red Sea was hot but calm, and the Marquis knew that they were making swift progress towards India.

He found also to his surprise that he looked forward to his conversations with Ankana, both at luncheon and at dinner.

He had never before been with an attractive woman who had not flirted with him with her eyes, her lips, her words, and every movement of her body.

Ankana, looking absurdly young with her long hair and shortened gowns talked to him as if she was the same age as he was.

She was, in fact, very much wiser on a number of subjects that the Marquis had never before discussed with a woman.

They talked about the religions of the East and the native customs in different countries they had both visited.

Here Ankana had read about, and actually knew considerably more than the Marquis did.

Inevitably they took different points of view.

The Marquis would think later in the evening that he might have been talking to one of his more intelligent men-friends at the Club.

Alternatively listening to a Statesmen at some Parliamentary dinner.

He thought it extraordinary that anyone so young should know so much.

Then he was aware of something he had not experienced before, namely that Ankana listened to what he said without trying to bring the conversation round to herself.

The Marquis had never before met a woman who could argue on a subject without making it entirely personal.

Also a woman who, if he did not agree with her, did not consider it an insult.

Ankana's mind seemed to flash like lightning from subject to subject.

The Marquis found a little ruefully, she would quickly find any weak spot in his argument, so that he had to concede that she was more often the winner than he was.

After he had gone to bed he would lie in the darkness thinking over what she had said.

He found himself trying to think of new subjects with which to confront her the following day.

Sometimes, unexpectedly, she would sit in silence and it was not because she had nothing to say.

It gave her a serenity which he liked and admired.

He guessed that it had something to do with her study of Yoga.

She had told him that Yoga appealed to her, as did the Buddhist philosophy, more than any other religion she had so far encountered on her travels.

It was certainly a very strange situation, the Marquis thought, for him to be in.

He knew how amused any of his friends would be if they knew of it.

They would find it impossible to believe that he had been alone for so long with a woman without making love to her, or being aware that she expected it.

It was quite obvious that Ankana expected nothing of the sort.

The Marquis was not even certain that she liked him.

He was just a means of getting her quickly to her father.

"Have you ever thought," he asked her one evening after dinner, "that in rushing away from London like this, you are spoiling your chances of finding yourself a suitable husband?"

Ankana looked at him in surprise.

"If you think that is why I agreed to be presented at Court, and was ready to attend the Balls and Receptions which Aunt Alice thought were so important, you are quite mistaken."

"Then what were you doing it for?" the Marquis asked.

"Papa told me it was what Mama would have wanted, if she had been alive, and I wanted to please him. But I have no intention of marrying, certainly not until I have seen a great deal more of the world."

Her voice lilted as she went on:

"Travelling with Papa is the most thrilling thing possible, and far more enjoyable than being with some stupid young man who has no thoughts beyond which horse will win the Gold Cup at Ascot, and if he will get invited to Marlborough House!"

The Marquis laughed.

"Not all men think only of those things!"

"I doubt if you are right!" Ankana said. "I have listened to Aunt Alice's friends talking in a derogatory way about their husbands and enthusing coyly over their lovers."

She paused and looked at him as she said sternly:

"I decided that any man who would waste his time with women like that must be half-witted!"

"And I suppose you have put me in that category," the Marquis observed.

Ankana looked at him as if she was surprised that he should have made the conversation personal.

Then tilting her head a little on one side she said:

"You are certainly far more intelligent than I expected, but I am astonished that you should waste your life in such a stupid way!"

"If you are judging me on hearsay," the Marquis said, "I consider that unfair, in England a man is innocent until he is proven guilty."

Ankana laughed.

"If you heard how the ladies talked about you, you would find them very persuasive witnesses for the prosecution!"

"Whatever they said should not have been said in front of you!" the Marquis said sharply.

"I doubt if they realised I was there," Ankana remarked. "I was only an unfledged, foolish débutante, and completly unimportant."

She paused to give a little laugh, before adding:

"That is of course unless I should marry somebody with a title and thereby become part of their small, inward-looking goldfish pond in which they reign supreme!"

"I think you are being a little hard on Society," the

Marquis said. "You forget that the men who rule the country and to whom it owe its greatness and prosperity must sometimes relax and be off-duty."

He paused before he said with a smile on his face:

"It is then they need the gentleness of a woman."

Ankana placed her elbows on the table and cupped her chin in her hands.

She looked up at him before she replied:

"I did not think of it from that point of view."

She put her head on one side and went on:

"What you are saying is that, having been concerned for so much of their time with political and national problems in the Houses of Parliament or in their Ministries, they do not want a woman to be clever, just soft and compliant."

"I think that sums it up very well."

"Papa said that if a man had any brains, he wanted to talk to the woman he loved as an equal. He loved Mama because she was clever as well as beautiful."

"Your father was talking of the one woman in his life who mattered to him," the Marquis said. "The women you are talking about – or rather, you listen to – are not speaking of their husbands, but they too are just looking for amusement."

Ankana sat back in her chair.

"I understand what you are saying," she said, "but I think it is wrong and rather unpleasant. Surely a man wants something different in his private life than just a pretty body?"

The Marquis thought this was an extraordinary conversation to be having with anyone so young.

Yet, as if he felt he must make her understand, he said quietly:

"I think all men seek the ideal woman whom he will marry and love, and with whom he is so content that he will have no desire to look in any other direction."

He gave a deep sigh and continued:

"Unfortunately, however, things do not always work out exactly as we want them to."

He searched for an illustration and went on:

"The flowers of today fade and wither and there is nothing one can do but throw them away and look again for another – rose, lily, or orchid."

He paused and then added:

"They are all beautiful in their own way, but are still perhaps not the perfection one is seeking."

There was silence until Ankana said:

"I understand what you are saying. But if somebody like you is seeking only perfection, will you not always be disappointed?"

"That is true," the Marquis replied, "but you would not expect me to stop looking? The stars are still up above, even though one cannot reach them."

Ankana thought for a moment, then to his surprise she said:

"Perhaps I . . misjudged you yesterday . . and of course I can only . . apologise."

"Thank you," the Marquis replied.

It was only after Ankana had gone to bed that he decided she was not being sarcastic.

He appreciated that she thought an apology was necessary.

"She is the most extraordinary girl I have ever met!" he told himself.

He fell asleep wondering what they would talk about the next day.

There had been changes in the Saloon since they had started out which the Marquis thought Ankana regarded with a twinkle in her eyes.

When they had left the Mediterranean there were three shining revolvers at the head of each sofa.

In a glass frieze above the windows there were nine

Winchester rifles which fired fifteen charges each without reloading and a magazine of ammunition in a cupboard by the books.

Four brass cannons had been rolled out on deck, as a defence against possible pirates in the China seas.

"We are hoping we shall not encounter any," the Marquis explained when Ankana exclaimed at the sight of so many weapons. "At the same time, I have learnt to be prepared."

He added seriously:

"I have no wish for my new yacht to be ransacked, besides the fact that pirates are very casual about whom they kill when they board a ship."

Ankana knew he was being sensible.

At the same time, she prayed that neither pirates nor anything else would prevent them from reaching Bangkok.

The night after they had passed the Southern point of India she thought she heard a shot.

Jumping out of bed she went to the port-hole in her cabin and drew back the curtains.

She could see nothing, then another shot came.

Although it seemed far away she was frightened and, going out of her cabin, she knocked on the Marquis's door.

When he did not answer, she opened it.

There were no lights and he was asleep.

Because he had lived with danger and also been a soldier, the mere fact that she was standing there, even though she did not call out, woke him.

When he could see her silhouetted against the light that was behind her in the passage, he sat up in bed.

"What is it?" he asked.

"I heard shots," Ankana replied, "and I am frightened in case it is pirates!"

"We will soon find out," the Marquis said. "Put on something warm and I will join you in a minute."

She had acted so quickly that she had not thought to put on her dressing-gown.

She had no idea that her slim body had been silhouetted against the light in the passage.

She went back to her cabin to obey the Marquis's instructions.

A few seconds later she heard him come from his cabin to join her.

He walked ahead of her up the companionway and onto the deck above.

He opened the door which led them outside under the awning.

When he crossed to the railing the light of the moon and the stars shimmering on the sea revealed that they were not far from the land.

The Marquis realised that they were rounding the South coast of Ceylon and that the shots Ankana had heard must have come from there.

Then there was another explosion in the distance, followed by several more.

He was sure that a battle of some sort was taking place either between two ships or perhaps a ship and the mainland.

Somewhat perturbed he hurried along the deck and onto the bridge where he found the Captain already there.

"Miss Brook was awakened by the shots," he said.

As he spoke he was aware that Ankana was beside him.

"I think, M'Lord," the Captain said, "it's pirates and the best thing we can do is to get away from them as quickly as possible!"

"I agree with you," the Marquis replied.

"I was just about to order the cannons to be manned," the Captain went on, "but it seems quiet enough ahead."

The Marquis looked and in the bright moonlight it was easy to see for some distance.

They reassuringly appeared to be the only ship in sight.

He realised the Captain was increasing speed and steering the '*Sea Horse*' away from the coast.

"I think we should be all right, Captain," the Marquis said, "but you had better take the precaution of doubling the night watch, at least for the next few hours."

"I'll do that, M'Lord."

Ankana said nothing, but as she stood beside him the Marquis realised she was apprehensive.

Without thinking he put out his hand to take hers.

He felt her fingers quiver and thought it was the first time she had shown any sign of fear.

He drew her away from the bridge and back to where they had stood at the railing to look out towards the explosions.

He was sure now from what he could see and hear that there were two ships firing at each other.

"It . . it might have been . . us," Ankana said in a frightened voice, "and that might have stopped us . . reaching Bangkok and Papa."

The Marquis did not point out that when they reached Bangkok her father was most unlikely to be there waiting for them.

Instead he said:

"We have been fortunate so far, and we can only be grateful that the pirate ship which was obviously lurking in these waters had its attention attracted in another direction."

"That is what I was thinking, too."

As Ankana spoke she threw her head back and looked up at the stars overhead.

She looked, as she did so, lovely in the moonlight.

The Marquis was aware he was still holding her hand, although he had the strange feeling that she had completely forgotten his existence.

"Are you thanking the gods who you believe are

watching over us?" he asked.

Although he spoke lightly, he was not mocking her.

"Of course!" she replied. "One must always be grateful and I am very, very grateful that your cannons are silent, and we have not had to take the revolvers from the Saloon."

"I suppose by that," the Marquis replied, "you are telling me you know how to use one?"

"Of course I do!" Ankana replied. "Papa taught me when I was quite small. As he said, one never knows when it might come in useful, as it might have been tonight."

"I too am very grateful," the Marquis said, "that it is not us, but somebody else who is battling with an enemy."

For a moment he felt Ankana's fingers tighten on his, before she said:

"I will go on praying that we shall arrive in Bangkok in safety. I have been praying so hard for Papa that I had forgotten that we too need protection."

She spoke quite seriously, as if she was rebuking herself.

Then she smiled up at the Marquis, and releasing her hand disappeared through the door opposite him.

For a moment he stared after her in surprise.

He had wanted to go on talking to her.

He thought wryly that it was unusual for any women to leave him before he had no further need of her.

He looked back to where there were still flashes of light from the now distant guns and found himself hoping that Ankana's prayers would be effective.

She had looked so lovely with her face turned up to the moonlight.

It was not hard to believe that she really was in touch with the gods who she said protected them, and the spirits who dwelt in the white-capped mountains.

Then he laughed at himself.

"If this journey goes on for much longer," he thought, "I shall find myself believing in magic, sorcery, witchcraft and, of course, in the Immortal gods on Olympus!"

He walked across the deck.

As he descended the companionway which led to the master cabin, the Marquis thought that, if nothing else, this was a strange and remarkable voyage.

And so far, surprisingly enough, he had not been in the least bored.

Chapter Four

The '*Sea Horse*' steamed up the Gulf of Siam.

The Marquis knew that the entrance to the river on which Bangkok was built was just ahead, and said to the Captain:

"I think we have beaten the record!"

"We certainly have, M'Lord!" the Captain replied. "We shall be anchoring outside the Palace on the Menam Chao Phya having taken only twenty days."

"That is excellent!" the Marquis said. "I congratulate you, Captain, and I am very grateful."

"Thank you, M'Lord," the Captain replied. "I'm rather pleased with myself for I thought when you first suggested it, it'd be impossible."

The Marquis was aware they had succeeded only because the yacht had steamed at full speed both by day and by night.

He knew now there was a great number of problems ahead of him, the first being Ankana.

As they entered the great river with its lighthouse standing alone outside, with sunken junks and other obstructions on each side of it, to keep out an enemy, he was aware of the excitement rising in her.

The yacht moved upstream and they saw the mangroves, the tall, feathery bamboos, and the stately palm trees interlaced with lianes and gigantic creepers.

There were also the boats which carried the fish to the Bangkok market.

These were distinguishable by their high stem and stern posts and long finely modelled lines, with queer Viking-type double rudders.

There were fishing craft of all sorts.

Children paddling their small canoes about the river, diving into the steamers' wash, calling and laughing and waving to the yacht as it went by.

There were too floating houses on their rafts.

Further up river there were wharfs and jetties, rice mills, and crowded rows of native rice-boats.

It was all, the Marquis thought, fascinating.

At the same time, he was aware that while Ankana was apparently watching what they were passing, she was tense with excitement.

At last they had arrived and would soon, as she believed, be able to find her father.

Because he was convinced it was a forlorn hope, the Marquis drew her into the Saloon saying:

"I want to talk to you, Ankana."

She looked at him with her huge dark eyes.

He thought uncomfortably that she was aware of what he was about to say before it reached his lips.

"When we arrive at Bangkok," he began, "I will go at once to the Palace to see the King and find out exactly what is the position as regards your father."

There was a little pause before Ankana said in a quiet voice:

"I am coming with you!"

"I think that would be a mistake," the Marquis answered quickly. "Perhaps the King will feel embarrassed by your presence and will not speak as frankly as he would have done without your being there."

"I understand exactly what you are saying to me,"

Ankana replied, "but I intend to accompany you, or if you prefer, I will ask for a private audience with the King."

She paused a moment before she went on firmly:

"I feel he will not refuse my father's daughter."

The Marquis's lips tightened as he knew she was being very obstinate.

Then because he felt it would be hopeless to go on arguing with her, he said:

"Very well, we will go there together."

His voice dropped as he said more sternly:

"But let me make this absolutely clear, Ankana: if there are any investigations to be made, if there is a chance of there being any danger, you will stay aboard the yacht."

He expected her to argue. Instead she laughed.

"Do you really think that I will agree to that?" she asked after a moment. "If you leave me here alone, I shall investigate if that is what is required, Papa's supposed death."

She smiled at him, and added:

"I dare say I shall be just as successful, or more so, than you will be."

"Now listen to me, Ankana," the Marquis said, "this is not a game!"

He looked at her sternly as he went on:

"As you are well aware, your father and I have been together before in very uncomfortable situations, and ones which would have certainly ended in disaster if you had been present."

"Now you are 'hitting below the belt'!" Ankana protested. "How can you be sure of that? Nor have you any right to assume that I would be an encumbrance rather than a help to you."

"Dammit!" the Marquis exclaimed. "You will do as you are told and stay on the yacht, if I have to lock you in your cabin!"

Ankana did not answer.

She merely smiled in what he thought was an infuriating manner, which brought him to the verge of losing his temper.

"The trouble with you," he said, "is that you have been spoilt. Your father has allowed you to have your own way."

He scowled at her before he went on:

"But as I have no wish to have you murdered in front of my eyes, or your blood on my hands, you will do as I say!"

"And why should I do that?" Ankana enquired.

"Because I will compel you!" the Marquis snapped.

Even as he spoke he knew it was very unlikely she would obey him.

What was more he really had no idea how he could force her to do so.

He turned angrily to the window to look out at the floating houses they were passing.

Then he heard her say behind him in a surprisingly soft voice:

"Please . . do not let us argue . . I am really very grateful to you for bringing me here, and all that . . really matters is that we find . . Papa."

The Marquis did not turn round, but after a moment he said in a very different tone from what he had used before:

"And suppose we do not find him?"

"Then . . you will be . . right and I will be . . wrong!" Ankana said very quietly.

An hour later they had their first sight of the spires of the Palace.

As they anchored outside its walls, the Marquis could see the gold of the Temples flashing in the sunshine, and the multiple-gabled roofs of the Palaces.

It was not long after they were anchored that he and Ankana went ashore.

Once they were inside the Palace itself, the picturesque buildings with their gilt horned roofs and the pinnacled pagodas seemed overwhelming.

They were met by a Chamberlain, or *Phaya*.

He wore a long white jacket with gold buttons, a purple silk *panung*, the strange loose breeches common to every man and woman in Siam, with white silk stockings and buckled shoes.

The Chamberlain said in understandable, if not good English, that he was astonished that the Marquis had managed to arrive so quickly.

He welcomed them both on behalf of His Majesty who, he said, would see them privately as soon as it was possible for him to do so.

In the meantime, they were taken to the Saranroum, or Palace of Calm Delights, where coffee-ices were brought to them.

The Chamberlain said that the Palace was at their disposal if the Marquis wished to stay there rather than on his own yacht.

The Marquis did not make a direct reply.

He thought perhaps it would be wise to find out first from the King exactly what had happened to Calvin Brook.

If, as he suspected, there was no doubt about his death, the sooner Ankana accepted it and was ready to leave Bangkok the better.

The Chamberlain had obviously informed the King immediately of their arrival.

They were actually not long in the Palace of Calm Delights before a servant came running with the information that His Majesty was ready to see them.

They were taken across the court-yard, where the sun was very hot, into the Chakri Palace where the Reception Rooms were decorated with portraits of previous Kings.

There was a small throne at one end of the room.

When King Chulalongkorn appeared, once he had entered the room the Chamberlain and all the other Courtiers who had accompanied him left.

Obviously His Majesty's instructions were that he was to be left alone with the Marquis and Ankana.

He was a handsome man, and besides being taller than most of the members of his family, was better-looking than any of them.

As the Marquis bowed, the King held out his hand and said:

"It is delightful to see you again, My Lord!"

"It is very gracious of Your Majesty to receive us," the Marquis replied, "and I am extremely grateful for Your Majesty's invitation to visit you even under such tragic circumstances."

The King looked at Ankana and the Marquis said:

"May I present, Your Majesty, Mr. Calvin Brook's daughter, Ankana, who wished to come with me and as you will understand I found it difficult to refuse her request."

"I have heard of you, Miss Ankana," the King said.

He was speaking excellent English, as he had done when he came to England.

Although he often used an interpreter because he was nervous of making mistakes.

With the Marquis he had always been very much at his ease.

He now suggested with a gesture of his hand that they should be seated in some stiff armchairs which were standing in the centre of the room.

Ankana thought it was strange that it had been arranged that they should sit so isolated as it were, in the middle of such a very large Reception-Room.

Then as the King lowered his voice she was aware that he had chosen this deliberately.

It would be impossible for anybody, even with very acute hearing, to overhear what he was saying.

He spoke first to Ankana as if he thought it correct to do so, saying:

"I must express Miss Ankana, how deeply distressed I

was when I was told of your father's death."

Ankana was looking at him.

The Marquis was aware from the expression in her eyes that she was looking deep beneath the surface in a strange way he had seen her do before.

Then after only a very slight pause, she replied:

"I appreciate, Your Majesty, your kind condolences, but I think you are aware, as I am, that they are unnecessary."

The King was still for a moment, then he said:

"Do you mean by that that you are doubting the report of your father's death?"

"That is what we are hoping Your Majesty will tell us," Ankana replied.

As if the Marquis thought she should make herself even more clear he said:

"Miss Brook is sure there is some mystery about her father's reported death, and in fact, she is convinced in her heart that he is alive!"

He could not although he tried, prevent his own doubt revealing itself in the way he spoke, and the King said in reply:

"The reason I asked you here, My Lord, was that I found the report of Mr. Calvin Brook's death somewhat mysterious."

He paused and smiled at the Marquis and went on:

"There is no one else I can ask but yourself to investigate whether what I have been told is the truth."

The Marquis settled himself a little more comfortably in his chair before he said:

"I can only ask Your Majesty to be frank with me, as you have been in the past."

"As you are well aware," the King replied, "I am extremely grateful to you for the help you have previously given Mr. Brook when he served us in ways which it would be a mistake to speak of now!"

He looked around him before he went on:

"If he is dead, then that will be a tragic loss for me personally, as well as for Siam."

He spoke with a sincerity which seemed to come from his heart.

As if Ankana was impatient to be done with the preliminaries she bent forward and glasping her hands together said:

"Please, Your Majesty, tell us what happened."

The King lowered his voice as he said:

"I asked your father to help me when I received notice from the Abbot of one of our most famous Temples in Chiang Mai that a priceless treasure which had been presented as a special gift had been stolen."

The Marquis had expected to hear something of the sort.

"You are of course, aware," the King went on, "that in many of our Temples where we have statues of the Lord Buddha we also have a very large imprint of his foot."

The Marquis knew this was true.

The foot of Buddha in Siam, like the statue itself, was usually covered by small pieces of gold leaf.

These were applied by the worshippers as they prayed, just as in a Roman Catholic Church candles were lit in front of the saints.

"A monk who originally came from Chiang Mai," the King continued, "had a vision which led him to find in our Gem Mines five priceless and unusually large blue sapphires."

He stopped speaking a moment, and then continued:

"These he conveyed to the Temple of Chiang Mai where they became the toe-nails on the foot of Lord Buddha, and had attributed them remarkable Holy powers which have been proved over and over again in the last five years."

Ankana was listening intently, her eyes on the King's face, and the Marquis saw her lips move as the King went on:

"Then they were stolen."

"How could that be possible?" the Marquis asked.
He knew that a treasure of such consequence would be guarded by the monks both by day and by night.
"Two monks were stabbed to death and the sapphires snatched away by men who must have managed to enter the Temple without arousing suspicion."
"And did this happen at night?"
"No, because then the Temple would have been locked and there would have been a guard on duty."
The Marquis looked surprised as the King went on:
"It happened early in the morning when the doors are first opened and usually there are few visitors, so the monks were not as alert as they would have been later in the day."
"What happened when it was known?" the Marquis asked.
"The Abbot was wise enough not to let the people of Chiang Mai know what had occurred and sent a special emissary to Bangkok immediately to inform me."
The King sighed before he continued:
"You are aware, My Lord, that there have been a number of difficult situations in the north of my country and in our relations with the Burmese."
He paused to smile at the Marquis before he added:
"If the people of Chiang Mai suspected that those who had been their old enemies were making trouble, we might have had many deaths on our hands, which would be a tragedy for the whole country."
"I agree with Your Majesty," the Marquis said.
He was well aware that Chiang Mai had for many years been a trouble spot until in the last century it had been finally accepted as being part of Siam.
"As soon as I heard what had happened," the King continued, "I sent for Mr. Brook and when I had explained our predicament he said he would do his best to find out what had happened to the five Holy sapphires, and if possible recover them."

The Marquis nodded as if that was what he would have expected, and the King continued:

"In the meantime I instructed the Abbot at Chiang Mai to pretend that the sapphires were still on the foot of the Lord Buddha."

The Marquis looked surprised and the King explained:

"Because of the holiness attributed to them, the gold leaf applied by those praying in the shrine had covered the previous stones completely, and the people will assume, although they cannot see them, that they are there."

"That was wise of Your Majesty," the Marquis said. "So Calvin Brook set off on the mission you had entrusted to him."

"Although I did not hear anything from him, I was not perturbed," the King replied, "until three weeks ago, before I telegraphed to our Ambassador in England, I was told that the body of Mr. Brook had been found in the river at Chiang Mai."

The King looked apprehensively as Ankana as he spoke as if he feared she might scream or faint.

As she did not move, her large eyes fixed on his face, His Majesty went on:

"The body had been in the water for a long time, and I understand the features were not recognisable."

He drew in his breath and continued:

"There were papers which told the fingers who he was, and on the little finger of one hand a signet-ring, which I have here with me."

The King drew the ring from a pocket of his embroidered coat, and putting it on the flat of his hand he held it out to Ankana.

She rose from her chair, knelt in front of him, and he gave her the ring.

She held it tightly in her hand and as she did so closed her eyes.

The Marquis was afraid for the moment that she was about to faint.

Then as he was silent and so was the King she opened her eyes and said:

"I know now . . with absolute certainty . . that Papa is alive!"

"Why should you say that?" the King asked.

Ankana sat back on her heels and looked up at him.

"For two reasons, Your Majesty," she replied. "First, Papa was alive when he took the ring from his finger and placed it on the dead man's."

She drew in her breath.

"Secondly, when Papa was in disguise, as I imagine he was when he went to Chiang Mai, he would not have been so foolish as to wear clothing which would have shown anybody who was spying on him who he actually was!"

Ankana spoke with a little note of triumph in her voice, and the King stared at her. Then he said:

"That makes sense to me! What do you think, My Lord?"

"I do not wish to raise Ankana's hopes unduly," the Marquis answered, "but I can only pray that somehow I can substitute her optimism and find that her father is alive."

The King smiled.

"That is what I hoped you would say. You know, My Lord, that any help I can give you, any assistance you need, is at your disposal. You have only to ask for it."

"I thank Your Majesty," the Marquis replied, "and I promise that I will do everything in my power both to find Calvin Brook and to bring you back the Holy sapphires."

The King rose to his feet and both the Marquis and Ankana rose too.

"I am very grateful for your help," the King said.

He spoke simply but the Marquis was aware how much it meant.

Then as there was no more to be said, Ankana curtsied, and the Marquis bowed.

The King walked across the Reception Room where, as he reached the door at the far end, it opened and he disappeared.

The Marquis looked at Ankana who was holding her father's signet-ring in her hand.

She was looking at it with what he thought was a very touching expression in her eyes.

However he did not say anything and the Chamberlain came hurrying back into the room to say fussily:

"Now does Your Lordship wish to stay in the Palace, or will you be returning to your yacht?"

"I think for the time being we will return to the yacht," the Marquis replied, "but I am very grateful to His Majesty for his generous offer of hospitality."

"Of course you will let me know if there is anything you require," the Chamberlain went on. "His Majesty's instructions are that your slightest wish is to be obeyed."

The Chamberlain bowed to the Marquis before continuing:

"Servants will be available and there will be sentries on duty where your yacht is at anchor."

"I can only thank you again," the Marquis said.

"If you wish to dine with His Majesty this evening, I think that can be arranged."

"I will think about it," the Marquis replied. "As you will understand, we have had a long voyage, and Miss Brook and I are both somewhat fatigued by the ceaseless movement of the waves."

The Chamberlain smiled.

"That I understand as I, My Lord, am a very bad sailor, except of course on the smooth waters of the river!"

Both men laughed, then as Ankana and the Marquis were escorted by one of the Chamberlain's assistants back to the yacht they did not speak until they reached it.

Only as they went into the Saloon did Ankana ask as if she could be silent no longer:

"What are you going to do? What are you planning?"

The Marquis sat down in a chair.

"Now, let us think this out very carefully."

"I am sure we must act quickly!"

"It is always a mistake to do anything without due consideration," the Marquis insisted.

He smiled at her before he added:

"If, as you think, your father is in hiding, to go blundering after him might result in his death as well as ours!"

There was a little silence before Ankana said:

"I am sure you are right, and I am being foolish. It is just that I am so worried about Papa."

"Suppose you tell me what you think has happened to him," the Marquis suggested.

He was sitting in an armchair and she sank down on the rug at his feet.

With her long hair falling over the shoulders of her simple muslin gown, she looked just as young as she was pretending to be.

The Marquis found himself thinking how admirably controlled she was.

He knew that most women of his acquaintance, faced with the same situation would be crying, clinging to him, and begging him to comfort them.

Alternatively they would be screaming hysterically that it would be a mistake to court danger and he must order somebody else to do his dirty work.

Ankana did not look at him.

Instead her eyes went to the sunshine outside the window of the Saloon.

He felt as if she drew from it some sort of help before she said in a low voice:

"I think . . Papa realised he was being . . followed. He

therefore knew he must . . disappear completely in order to convince those who were . . spying on him that he was no longer . . there."

She paused and, as if she was seeing what had happened with an inner eye, she went on:

"He found a dead man in the river, which is not surprising, for I believe it often happens in this part of the world."

She smiled as she went on:

"It would be easy for him to plant clothing which would be discovered later and to make it even more convincing put his signet-ring on the dead man's finger."

The Marquis said quietly:

"I agree that that is what may have happened. Do you think your father is still in Chiang Mai?"

"If the stones had already been taken from the Temple, the thief would not hang about," Ankana replied.

"There again I agree with you," the Marquis said. "I think personally the stones are most likely to be on their way back from Chiang Mai to where they came from."

Ankana stared at him before she asked in astonishment:

"Why should you think that?"

"The monk who had the vision and found them in the first place took them to where he had originally come from. But knowing how deeply the Siamese feel about anything that is holy and is attributed to Buddha."

He shook his head before he continued:

"I cannot help feeling that the people in Chan Chantrabrat which as you know, is the Gem district of Siam, would resent anything so specially precious being taken from there."

Ankana clasped her hands together.

"That is clever of you . . very clever! So you do not think it was the Burmese who stole the stones?"

The Marquis shook his head.

"It is much more likely to be those who control the

digging in the mines and are extremely possessive of what they find."

He paused a moment, and then added:

"They would, I am sure, resent anything so unusual being taken away to another part of the Kingdom which did not even belong to Siam until the end of the last century."

"I am sure you are right in that supposition," Ankana agreed, "but where do you think we will find Papa?"

"Although I have certainly not your clairvoyant powers," the Marquis said a little mockingly, "I imagine he will be looking in the South, and not in the North."

"Then what shall we do?" Ankana enquired.

"First," the Marquis said, "I am going to see a friend of mine who is actually a very much older friend of your father's."

He stopped to think a moment before he went on:

"She is a lady who has helped us both in the past, and who knows almost everything that happens in Bangkok and in other parts of the country as well!"

"It sounds as though she might be helpful," Ankana agreed. "Can we visit her now?"

The Marquis smiled.

"It is definitely not a question of 'We'," he said. "I must go alone to see Beebe and you will stay here!"

"That is most unfair! You know I must go with you!" Ankana replied angrily.

"You bullied me into letting you come with me to see the King," the Marquis said, "but now I am afraid you simply must accept my assurance that it is really impossible for you to meet Beebe."

"Why?" Ankana asked in a hostile voice.

"Because her house is a place in Bangkok where only men can go," the Marquis replied. "I think you are intelligent enough to realise there are places of amusement which are barred to women."

He smiled at her before adding:
"Especially to one who happens to be a Lady."
Ankana stared at him, then she asked:
"Do you mean . . there are places which are . . improper?"
She hesitated before the last word and the Marquis said:
"As I have already told you, there are places of amusement that are only for men. The only women there are girls provided by Beebe and they certainly would not tolerate any competition!"
The Marquis chose his words with care, for he knew he had to make quite certain that Ankana did not follow him.
Beebe kept what was a Palace of Pleasure, very much the same as could be found in Paris and, to a lesser degree, in all the Capital cities of Europe.
Ankana walked to the window and after a moment she said:
"I have heard of such places, but I cannot understand sombeody like you . . or Papa . . wishing to . . visit them!"
"As I have already said," the Marquis replied, "we have been in the unique position of getting information from Beebe that would have been quite unobtainable from anybody else in the City."
He paused a moment and then continued:
"On one occasion for instance, through her guidance we discovered before he was able to do any damage, a man who was intent on murdering the King."
"You mean . . he was an anarchist?" Ankana asked in a note of horror.
"He came from Europe where the Police were hot on his trail," the Marquis said. "We found him in Bangkok and were instrumental in having him captured and taken to Germany where he was tried and executed for the murder of a Grand Duke."
Ankana drew in her breath. Then she said:

"I understand now, and you must have thought me very stupid not to have realised it before, that those sort of places could be useful in an emergency like this."

"They are places of which you would have no knowledge," the Marquis said, "if you were behaving as you should, and enjoying life as a débutante."

"Now you are definitely trying to make me feel uncomfortable and humiliated," Ankana protested. "It is just that . . I do not like to think of . . Papa or you . . coming in contact with women like that."

The words seemed to be jerked from her lips.

Because she looked so innocent and pure as she spoke the Marquis had an almost irrepressible desire to put his arms around her.

He wanted to tell her he would protect her not only from anything that was dangerous, but also from anything that was unpleasant, that might besmirch or sully her.

Then as she looked at him and their eyes met, Ankana said to him in a hesitating little voice:

"Y.you will . . take care of . . yourself?"

She did not know why she said it, but the Marquis understood and he said:

"I shall not be away any longer than I can help, and when I come back, perhaps I shall have news of your father."

"I do hope so!" Ankana replied.

She left him and went below to her cabin.

Alone she found herself thinking of her father and how vital it was that they should get in touch with him quickly.

She was also thinking of the Marquis and how much she disliked his going to a place that was unpleasant and degrading.

Because the thought of his being with women who would offer him what they thought of as 'delights' and which Ankana had heard some men found very appealing, she felt as if there was a pain in her breast.

Although she tried to put it away, she had the feeling it

would remain there until the Marquis returned from Beebe.

It was a place which she was sure was something like those referred to in the Bible as 'Sodom and Gomorrah'.

Because she was in fact tired and had found the moist heat when they had walked to the Palace and back again somewhat exhausting, Ankana lay on her bed.

She did not wish however to sleep because she wanted to see the Marquis as soon as he returned.

Thinking about him, she realised how kind he had been to her these last weeks.

How interesting it had been to talk to him as they had done at mealtimes.

Although she had loved talking to her father she realised that the Marquis's mind worked in a different way from his.

It had been fascinating to discover what he thought about so many subjects that interested her.

They had taken opposite views on most subjects.

They argued without coming to agreed conclusions, but enjoyed the stimulus it gave their brains.

Ankana would go to bed thinking out new subjects she would raise with the Marquis the next day and perhaps surprise him because she was so well-informed.

It was impossible for her not to realise how handsome he was.

Although she had sneered at him for being conventional and materially-minded, she was uneasily aware that where she was concerned he was almost uncannily perceptive.

He would know what she was thinking, even when she was trying to hide her thoughts from him.

At the same time he was part of the Social World to which ever since she had been in London she had taken an instinctive dislike.

One reason for this was that it entailed separation from her father.

Another was that she thought it a waste of time entertaining the people her aunt thought were so important simply because they had a title, or were wealthy.

With her father as her ideal, she thought a life of exploring or visiting strange countries and often facing danger was entrancing.

She could not understand how women could be content with fussing over their gowns and trying to make themselves look more beautiful than their Creator intended.

They wanted to flirt with every man who came within their orbit, whether he was married or single, old or young.

"It is all such a waste of time," she told herself.

Now, having been with the Marquis for nearly three weeks, she could understand why women pursued him.

Why to think they had captured him, even for a short while, as a 'feather in their caps', which entitled them to crow over the other women whom he had ignored.

She did not know why she had suddenly begun to understand so much that she had despised before.

Yet at the back of her mind she could never forget that he had worked with her father and her father had admired him.

However, wastefully, he might spend his time with stupid people, she was aware that he was very influential and extremely well read.

She was aware too that he had, although she had tried not to admit it, a forceful personality.

It would have made him listened to and admired even if he had not been a man both of rank and of wealth.

Now he was going to a place which catered for different amusements than those enjoyed in his social life and from which she was completely excluded.

Because she was always honest with herself, she knew that what she was feeling, was extraordinarily enough, jealousy!

She could imagine, although she was not sure, that

women like Beebe would put their arms around him.

They would be familiar in a way no Lady would be in public.

Perhaps they would kiss him!

The thought of his firm, rather hard lips kissing a beautiful Siamese woman, or perhaps a Chinese girl, made Ankana feel murderous.

There was no other word for it.

Suddenly she knew she would want to exterminate any woman who attracted the Marquis simply because she was a woman.

"What is wrong with me that I should think like this?" Ankana asked herself.

Darkness came and there was only the passing light from barges on the river to flicker through her uncurtained porthole.

She realised it was growing late and the Marquis had not yet returned.

It was then, as her whole being yearned for him and she tried with her thoughts to draw him back, she knew that she loved him.

Chapter Five

When the Marquis left Ankana, he hired a carriage.

He gave the driver the address of what was one of the most notorious places of interest to tourists in all Bangkok.

There were, he knew, few places like it except in Paris.

Beebe had created a very special house of Pleasure for every man who visited the Capital of Siam.

She was, as the Marquis knew, unique.

While her father had been French and her mother Siamese, she had been given a Cosmopolitan education and had travelled in many countries of Europe.

Then she came back to Bangkok to set up first only in a small way a Bordello that was different from those that existed at the time.

The Siamese had been famous for many years for their skill in massage.

Elderly people came from far and wide to Bangkok for treatment for their aches and pains.

Beebe transformed massage into a seductive and sensual source of pleasure for men.

She combined with it many other sorts of entertainment that they could not obtain anywhere else.

The Marquis had visited her house in the past.

He thought now when he arrived that it was even more luxurious and enticing than it had been before.

It was arranged in surprisingly good taste, with enough

Siamese ornamentation to make it seem Eastern and exotic to foreigners.

When he arrived, the porter who answered the door informed him that it was too early and he would have to come back again later.

When the Marquis explained that he was calling on Beebe as a personal friend, he was shown into a small, comfortable Sitting-Room.

It was where a man could if he wished, talk to a woman before he made up his mind what joys she should show him.

After only a few minutes a servant, dressed in an elaborate Siamese uniform which would not have seemed out of place in the Palace, took him to Beebe's private room.

This, as the Marquis knew, was where she saw her personal friends.

It was not open to gentlemen who were only interested in what was obtainable in the other parts of the establishment.

As he entered, Beebe looking very attractive, gave a cry of delight and holding out both her hands said:

"*Mon Cher!* I am so pleased to see you!"

Beebe spoke many languages, but although her English was good, she felt more at home in French.

As the Marquis was bilingual he answered her in that tongue.

"I am sure you expected me," he said.

He wanted to find out if she knew about Calvin Brook, and he was not surprised when she replied:

"Is it true that your friend is dead?"

"So you *have* heard that!" the Marquis exclaimed.

Beebe nodded and said:

"A friend who is very discreet arrived from Chiang Mai several days ago and informed me that it is whispered there that Mr. Brook was drowned, but no one is quite certain if it is true."

The Marquis sat down in a comfortable chair.

"That is why I have come to see you."

"A little bird told me that the King was expecting you."

The Marquis laughed.

"Can anything happen in this country without your knowing about it?"

"I sincerely hope not!" Beebe replied. "Otherwise fine gentlemen like yourself would not find me so useful!"

"I suspect that most 'fine gentlemen', as you call them, have other reasons for visiting you!" the Marquis said cynically.

Beebe made an expressive little gesture that was very French.

"*Oui, oui!* At the same time, although they are welcome, they are not important."

The Marquis had been aware for a long time that Beebe was part of the espionage system which was vital to Siam.

Since they had many enemies although they had managed to remain unconquered by any other country.

This however had not been achieved without sacrifice.

The King had been forced to give up 120 thousand square kilometres of disputed frontier territory.

But that had seemed a small price to pay for obtaining peace and the independence of the Siamese heartland in the Menam Chao Phya Basin.

There was an interruption as a servant came in with a tray of refreshment for the Marquis.

There was a bottle of French champagne besides a long and, he knew, excellent fruit drink which he preferred.

The drinks were offered to Beebe, but she waved them away and when they were alone again the Marquis said:

"You know that I have come here to ask you for information and help, for you of all people realise it would be a tragedy if we have really lost Calvin Brook."

"I agree with you there," Beebe said, "and I have something which I think will please you."

She rose from where she was sitting with an exquisite grace which was typical of the Siamese.

Her gown fitted her slim figure as if she was poured into it.

As she walked to her desk the Marquis appreciated how very pretty and attractive she was, although she must, he thought, be over thirty-five.

As was true of all Siamese women, the moisture in the air kept her complexion clear and unlined.

Beebe had a small, short nose which was characteristic of the Siamese, and a full curved provocative mouth.

She had inherited from her father her large dark eyes which sparkled when she talked.

It was impossible for her to look at a man without flirting with him in a manner which invariably evoked a response in him.

She took something from her desk, and walked back to where the Marquis was sitting.

She put her hands behind her back and asked:

"What will you give me if I solve your problem for you?"

"What are you asking?" the Marquis enquired. "Half my fortune?"

Beebe laughed.

"I have never been particularly interested in money where you are concerned, *Mon Brave.*"

"Then you know the answer to your question," the Marquis replied.

She gave him a very inviting look from under her long lashes, then without further provocation she held out to him what was in her hand.

He took it from her and to his surprise he saw it was a postcard.

It was a cheap, brightly-coloured picture of the Royal Barge which could be bought anywhere in Siam.

He looked at it for a moment, then turned it over and saw it was addressed to 'Lady Beebe', and written in English.

On the same side of the postcard was written:

"Having a restful time in Pattaya. Wish you were here. Tell 'Ossy' when you see him the fishing is good.
C."

The Marquis drew in his breath, then he asked:
"When did you receive this?"
"About a week ago."
"How right I was in knowing you would be able to help me!"
As he spoke he was looking at the postcard and finding it hard to believe his eyes.
He knew, although the hand-writing was deliberately unformed and somewhat of a scribble, that it was from Calvin Brook.
If he doubted that, the message for 'Ossy' was a convincing clue.
The simple reason was that when he and Calvin had come to Beebe's house in the past, the girls had asked their names.
They were not so indiscreet as to expect surnames from any of their customers.
When the Marquis, and he had not then inherited the title, had replied 'Osmond', they found it impossible to pronounce.
"We say 'Ossy'!" they had replied in their broken English, and as Ossy he was known, even to Beebe when she wished to tease him.
"Where is Pattaya?" he asked aloud.
"A small fishing village," she replied, "a little way down the coast South-East from Bangkok."
The Marquis put the postcard into his pocket and said:
"Thank you, Beebe, and you know if I find Calvin Brook how very grateful I shall be."
"And so will the King," Beebe said quietly.
She sat down close to him and taking his hand in hers she said:

"Now you are here, I want you to see the improvements I have made since your last visit and to talk to the new girls I have engaged."

She paused to smile at him before continuing:

"They are noted as being the most beautiful and of course the most skilful in the whole country."

"How could I expect anything else?" the Marquis asked. "But first, tell me about yourself."

He knew after she had helped him and given him exactly what he wanted, it would have been both rude and unkind to leave her.

He had to show his appreciation of her, both as a friend and as a woman.

He was, in fact, amused by the new joys that he found installed in what he learnt had now been renamed "*The Palace of a Thousand Delights*".

There were warm baths in which a man could soak away the tensions of the day, attended by the most alluring maidens who looked like mermaids.

Inside the massage rooms there were small Siamese women who kneeded every muscle on every part of the body with their tiny, sensitive fingers.

They also walked on the backs of their clients, massaging a man's spine with their toes.

In another larger room there were dancers, exotic and provocative.

They were partially dressed in the exquisite traditional embroidered garments that were part of Siamese history.

These and a dozen more delights Beebe showed the Marquis.

Then as she asked him with a rising of her wing-like eye-brows if he would like to participate in any of them, he replied:

"I would rather talk to you, and you know I am really interested in what you have been doing."

She knew to what he referred and took him back to her Sitting-Room.

While he sipped an excellent champagne she talked of the country, the King and the new and revolutionary reforms which were taking place, as if she herself was a Statesman.

She told him how the King's sons had returned from their European Schools.

This helped him to modernise the Army and Navy, while one of them had become Siam's First Minister of Justice.

The Marquis learnt that the first hospital, Sirira, had been opened after years of opposition.

"That is certainly an innovation!" he exclaimed.

Beebe laughed.

"The ordinary folk still prefer herbal remedies to *Farang* medicine and of course at first there was a great shortage of qualified doctors."

The Marquis laughed.

"That certainly made things difficult!"

"Nothing daunted the King," Beebe went on, "and when he returned from his European tours, where he told me that he met you, it gave him new ideas, so that he has built the Dlisit Palace on the site of the fruit orchard."

"What happens there?" the Marquis asked.

"His Majesty holds intimate parties, fancy-dress Balls, and often cooks the food himself."

The Marquis threw back his head and laughed.

"That is certainly something very strange and I should have thought would be considered most reprehensible on the part of a Siamese King. His ancestors must be horrified!"

"Some people are a little shocked," Beebe agreed, "but as the country prospers and even the peasants are better off then they have ever been, it is difficult to criticise him."

"He is certainly very much in advance of his time," the

Marquis said, "and since he has absolute power, if Siam can only remain at peace, then all other reforms are possible."

"That is what I believe," Beebe said, "and that is why I work for the King and this country because it is of importance to the whole world."

Beebe was speaking with a seriousness which the Marquis knew would have been very surprising to the majority of the men, however distinguished they were, who visited her house.

He suspected, as Calvin Brook had, that she was not only of vital use to the King politically but close to him.

That, if it is known would seem extremely reprehensible to the world outside.

His Majesty kept a close watch on those who had tried to make trouble for Siam in the past and were likely to do so again.

But he continued to sweep away the restrictions and errors of the past.

He was determined to put in their place a progressive policy which was essential if Siam was to survive.

The construction of the first railway and the first telegraph houses had begun seven years ago.

Now their usefulness was accepted, and people were no longer astonished by them.

There was so much more to come.

Agents like Beebe were essential if there was to be no more trouble on the borders of the country.

In fact, no revolutionary plotting and planning against the throne was possible without the King being aware of it.

The Marquis was so much enjoying talking to Beebe that it was after nine o'clock before he finally rose to his feet and said:

"I must go back."

"You are not staying at the Palace?"

"As I knew I was coming to see you, I refused His

Majesty's most kind invitation."

"Then, if you are free – must you go?"

He had risen to his feet and Beebe had risen too.

She was very small, her head hardly reaching his shoulder.

She looked very attractive and very exotic as she gazed up at him, standing close, and yet not touching him.

"I would like to stay," the Marquis said quietly, "but I have with me, as I expect you already knew, Calvin Brook's young daughter, and she will be waiting."

He saw the disappointment in Beebe's eyes.

Then as he bent his head to kiss her hand, her lips were against his cheek.

"You, *mon cher*, are the most attractive, the most charming, the most fascinating man I have ever met!" she said softly.

She was wearing an Eastern perfume which reminded the Marquis of the past.

Then as he said nothing but hesitated, Beebe said:

"I know the real reason you are leaving is that you wish to be moving as quickly as you can towards Pattaya, and I suppose your duty must come first."

The words as well as the voice were very moving, and the Marquis kissed her hand again before he replied:

"That is true, Beebe, but we shall meet again, and if I cannot find Calvin, as I hope I shall with your help, then I shall return."

She kissed his cheek again and he felt the softness of her lips on his skin.

Then with a quick change of mood that was characteristic of her she said:

"Take care of yourself. The girls in the South are very alluring and I shall be exceedingly piqued if they hold you as I am unable to do!"

"Anything you may hear from your spies in that particular will definitely be untrue!"

The Marquis's eyes were twinkling, and Beebe laughed as she said:

"Could anything be untrue which concerns you and a beautiful woman? Is Calvin's daughter as attractive a woman as he is a man?"

"Perhaps that would be impossible!" the Marquis parried. "She is as yet very young and women undoubtedly improve with age!"

"I appreciate the compliment," Beebe replied.

She let him out through a side-door so that he was not seen.

He was well aware, now that the doors were open, men were hurrying into the other part of the house, eager to sample the 'thousand delights' which Beebe offered them.

The carriage in which he had arrived was waiting.

As he drove back to the yacht, he thought how exceedingly lucky he had been.

Calvin, like his daughter, was perceptive enough to know that if he came to Bangkok to look for him, he would undoubtedly visit Beebe.

It was after half-past-nine, as he walked up the gang-plank.

Dobson was waiting for him.

He somewhat reproachfully hurried him down to his cabin where his evening-clothes were waiting, as was his bath.

The Marquis however waited until the door was shut. Then he said:

"Find the Captain, Dobson, and tell him that in an hour's time he is to move slowly and as unobtrusively as possible down river."

He looked about him before he went on:

"I do not want it to appear as if the yacht is hurrying away or that we are doing anything but finding another anchorage."

"I understands, M'Lord."

"Speak to the Captain alone, and do not let anybody else hear you," the Marquis ordered.

As Dobson hurried away he began to take off his clothes.

He thought that after the heat of the day and the humidity a cold bath would be more of a delight than anything Beebe could offer him.

He knew he must not hurry, since it would be a mistake for even the stewards to think there was any need for haste.

Later, when they were moving down river, there would be no one to question their destination or their purpose.

When he went above and entered the Saloon it was to find Ankana waiting for him.

As soon as he looked at her face he knew that she was upset.

"I am sorry if I am late," he said, "and I am sure you are hungry. But I met some friends and we started talking about the old days, and it was difficult for me to get away."

He knew that she would understand that he could not speak of her father since two stewards were in the Saloon waiting on them.

One of them handed the Marquis a drink, the other brought in the first course and set it down on a sideboard.

The Marquis walked to his place at the head of the table.

"You have not yet told me," he said conversationally, "what you thought of the Palace. Tomorrow I must take you to see the Emerald Buddha, which is one of the great sights of the world."

Ankana did not answer and he went on telling her what she knew already, that the Emerald Buddha was carved from one piece of jade.

It was an object of national veneration, and crowds would pour into the Chapel Royal to pay their respects to Buddha and his teachings, whenever it was open to the public.

"I expect you know that the Emerald Buddha was first

discovered in 1464," the Marquis went on as the stewards served them with a dish of fresh prawns.

It was followed by Pomfret, a Siamese fish unobtainable in any other part of the world.

Served with the sweet and sour sauce so beloved of the Chinese it was delicious.

There were several more courses to follow.

Only when the stewards had left the room and he and Ankana were at last alone did she say breathlessly:

"Did you find out anything? I must know!"

The Marquis smiled.

"I am aware of how curious you have been all through dinner," he said, "but it is of the utmost importance that even those in my employment and whom I trust should not have any idea what I have discovered or where we are going."

He saw a light appear in Ankana's eyes as she asked in a very low voice:

"What have you . . discovered?"

The Marquis drew the postcard which Beebe had given him from his pocket and handed it to her.

She read it slowly.

Then as he felt her whole body vibrate with excitement she turned her head to look at him, and he said:

"You were right, and of course I am ready to apologise for doubting you."

"Papa is at Pattaya," she said beneath her breath.

The Marquis thought it was like the lilting cry of a bird flying high in the sky.

He did not speak and after a moment she asked:

"Are we going . . there?"

As she spoke the Marquis felt the engines start up and the anchor being wound in.

"We are leaving now," he said, "but I want it to appear that we are merely moving to a quieter place to stay the night. No one will realise until the morning that we have actually left Bangkok."

"You think such precautions are important," Ankana murmured.

He knew it was more of a statement than a question.

"There is no need for me to answer that," he said. "As you yourself have said, your father is in danger and if, as I believe he has found the sapphires, then he will need our help."

He knew as he spoke, Ankana was tense, but he went on:

"We must appear to be quite ordinary visitors to Siam, staying in Pattaya because it is a convenient stopping-place on a voyage which will take us further East."

He paused to think for a moment and then added:

"I think Hong Kong might be a likely place for us to be making for."

Ankana drew in her breath.

"I understand!"

She looked down at the postcard before she handed it back to the Marquis.

It was then that the stewards came in to clear the table and the Marquis, putting the postcard back in his pocket said:

"Let us go out on deck. The river can be lovely at night with the lights reflected on the water."

They stood against the railing watching the houses on stilts as they moved past them.

Their lights were shimmering on the water and the strange vegetation that was always to be found in the Menam River was being disturbed in the wake of the yacht.

Then as Ankana stood beside him watching, as he thought, everything that passed, she said unexpectedly:

"Is she . . very lovely?"

For a moment the Marquis could not think to whom she was referring.

Then despite his considerable experience with women he was aware that Ankana was interested in a way he did not understand.

"I presume you are speaking of Beebe," he replied, "and I know you are as grateful to her as I am. The answer to your question is 'Yes', although perhaps the right word is 'fascinating'."

He was speaking almost as much to himself as Ankana.

He was thinking how unusual it was to find such a brilliantly intelligent woman in an age-old profession which was concerned more with the body than the mind.

"She is half French," he went on, "and I understand, although of course it may be an exaggeration, that her father was a young Diplomat."

He paused a moment and then went on:

"He left her mother with little or no money, and Beebe had to make her own way in the world."

"If she is so . . clever," Ankana remarked, "why does she have to . . live in what . . you call . . 'a House of Pleasure'?"

"Actually it is now called "*The Palace of a Thousand Delights*" the Marquis said with a note of amusement in his voice. "It is unique in Bangkok, and Beebe is the sort of person who would be appreciated in any country."

"Because . . she is so . . attractive?" Ankana asked.

"No, no, of course not!" the Marquis said. "Attractive and beautiful women are two a penny, but Beebe has an astute brain and a remarkable talent for espionage."

He stopped speaking a moment and then said:

"It has been helpful to your father as well as to Siam."

Ankana did not speak, but she moved nearer to the railing.

She leant against it staring with what the Marquis realised were unseeing eyes, as they passed a Temple with lights illuminating its grounds.

A moment later they passed a small tug drawing five

huge barges filled with vegetables.

The Marquis was still pre-occupied with the information Beebe had given him.

He was therefore surprised when Ankana asked him in a strange little voice that seemed to be propelled from her lips:

"Why were . . you so . . long? What . . else did you . . discover . . or did you stay . . with her because . . you enjoyed it?"

The Marquis turned his head to stare at her.

Then as he wondered why she had asked that question rather than talk of her father and how they could save him, she went on furiously:

"How can you . . degrade yourself and spend . . so long with women like that? How can . . you enjoy a . . thousand delights when you should have been . . thinking only of . . saving Papa?"

Her eyes were blazing as she continued:

"I was . . right! You are . . horrible and I . . hate you!"

She seemed almost to spit the words at him.

As the Marquis stood still in sheer astonishment, she ran away from him through the door by which they had come out on deck and he heard her footsteps going down the companionway.

For a moment he could not understand what had upset her.

Why after he had shown her the postcard from her father she should be thinking of anything else.

Then, although it seemed astonishing, he knew the answer.

He had not endured many scenes of reproaches and recriminations without knowing they were the signs of jealousy in a woman who loved him.

He was sure that Ankana did not understand at all the meaning of the word 'love' and was as completely innocent as she appeared to be.

Yet he could understand that, having been with him alone for three weeks, she resented his attention being focused on another woman.

Especially he told himself, when he was, as she had thought, so united with him in an overwhelming determination to save her father.

It seemed unnecessary however, for her to be upset.

The Marquis debated with himself whether he should go below and talk to her.

He wanted to assure her that absolutely nothing was more important in his mind than that he should find her father.

He would tell her she was accusing him unjustly when she thought he had stayed at "*The Palace of a Thousand Delights*" for other reasons than to have a most useful and informative conversation with Beebe.

But he thought she might rage at him, and the one thing he heartily disliked was a scene.

It was absurd that he should have to justify himself to a child who had forced herself upon him.

Once he had found Calvin Brook she would simply pass out of his life and that would be the end of the matter.

The yacht began to increase speed now and it was well away from the Palace.

He found himself thinking how extraordinary it was that Ankana, who had been so self-controlled and calm all the way to Bangkok, should suddenly become hysterical when he least expected it.

He could understand that she had been tense with anticipation of any news that he might bring back from Beebe.

Yet all through the voyage until now she had behaved in such an admirable fashion.

He had admired her serenity and it seemed incredible that now, for no apparent reason she should be in such a state.

He told himself firmly, as he had said to Ankana, that no

Lady should know anything about Houses of Pleasure or women like Beebe.

If by some mischance they learnt about them they should be dignified.

It was correct to pretend not to understand what was implied or why men were interested in them.

"The whole trouble is," he told himself, "that I do not understand young girls, nor do I want to, for that matter."

Then he thought of the sophisticated women whose favours he had enjoyed in London.

He knew, as he did so, if he was honest, that if any of them had come on this voyage with him, he would by this time, have been utterly bored.

They would have had no conversation about anything except themselves, and of course, him.

Certainly the fascinating arguments on obscure subjects which had kept Ankana and him talking and duelling with each other in words every evening would never have taken place.

He had to admit that throughout their voyage through the Mediterranean, the Red Sea, into the Indian Ocean and the Gulf of Siam he had never been bored for one minute.

What was more, his brain had been more active and more lively than it had been for a long time.

It seemed ridiculous that anyone as young as Ankana could stimulate his thoughts!

She had forced him to conclusions that had never crossed his mind until they had talked to each other.

That was the truth, and never had he thought her, as most women were, until this moment, aggressively feminine or tiresomely illogical.

"I expect she is just over-tired," he told himself, "and with her active imagination she may suspect Beebe of being very different from what she really is."

He thought perhaps Ankana's idea of a 'House of

Pleasure', was the sort of grotesque horror portrayed by Hogarth in his cartoons.

Then he asked himself how he could be expected to know the workings of a young girl's mind?

It all came back to the same thing – he should not have Ankana with him.

If he had had any sense, he would not have told her tonight where he was going.

He had in fact, grown used to talking and discussing things with her, not as a woman, but as if she was another man.

Now he knew a little belatedly that she was not only extremely intelligent but very, young and very vulnerable.

The knowledge that he had been in what the English might describe as a 'Bawdy House', and in the company of what the Bible called a 'harlot', would undoubtedly disturb her much more than it would the average girl of her age who would not know what it was all about.

"It was very stupid of me not to have said I was going to a Men's Club, or something of the sort," the Marquis told himself.

Once again he thought he would like to explain that nothing had taken place that need disturb her.

Then a sudden obstinacy made him think crossly that he would do nothing of the sort.

Because he wanted to distract his mind he went up onto the bridge.

He found the Captain at the wheel.

There were two seamen also in attendance and he waved them outside the Bridge House before he said:

"Now that we have got away, Captain, I want you to go full speed ahead for Pattaya and with any luck, we should reach there early tomorrow morning."

The Captain indicated a chart that was lying open in the Bridge House.

The Marquis pointed out Pattaya which proclaimed its

unimportance by being printed in very small letters.

Chanthaburi the centre of the Gem district was clearly indicated some way further down the coast.

The Marquis however, thought there would be no need to go further than Pattaya.

He was sure that once they arrived Calvin Brook would somehow get in touch with him.

It was an elating thought.

Having left the Captain about half-an-hour later he decided he would retire to bed.

He wanted to be up as early as possible to see the yacht arrive at Pattaya.

At least, he told himself, he had not wasted much time.

"A record run from London to Bangkok, and now within a day of my arrival I have a direct clue to Calvin's whereabouts!"

He paused and smiled to himself.

"It would have been impossible for anybody else to do things so swiftly."

He appreciated before he went below that the Captain understood they should not draw attention to themselves.

The lights in the Saloon had all been extinguished.

The yacht, while distinguishable by the required navigation lights, would not as she moved down river be in any way ostentatious.

"So far so good!" the Marquis thought as he walked along the passage to his cabin.

Then as he passed the cabin next door which was Ankana's he thought he heard a strange sound.

He stopped to listen, and heard to his astonishment that Ankana was crying.

He hesitated, until on an impulse he knocked on her door.

Instantly the sound he had heard stopped.

As Ankana did not answer he walked in.

There was only one small shaded light by the bed.

The curtains which fell from the ceiling on either side of the pillows made it difficult to see Ankana clearly.

Then she asked in a choked little voice:

"W.what . . do you . . want?"

The Marquis closed the door behind him.

He walked to the side of the bed, but Ankana did not move and he knew she was afraid that he should see her tears.

He sat down on the mattress facing her, and said quietly:

"I wanted to tell you that we are now steaming as quickly as possible towards Pattaya. I think we should be there tomorrow morning, perhaps very early."

Ankana did not answer and he had the feeling that she was finding it impossible to speak.

Then he asked in a kind voice:

"What has upset you?"

As he spoke he reached out his hand and covered one of hers that was lying on the linen sheet.

"You have been so brave and so self-controlled until now," he went on, "and I am sure your father would not wish you to break down at the last moment."

He felt Ankana's hand stiffen beneath his, but he did not release it.

After a moment she said in a small childlike voice:

"I . . I am sorry I . . was . . rude."

"It is understandable," the Marquis said. "You had to wait for a long time for my return."

He stopped speaking and smiled at her before he continued:

"I know you must have felt it agonising not knowing whether I had learnt something about your father or if we would have to seek for him blindly without any help."

As if the kind way in which he spoke swept away her unhappiness she turned her hand over and her fingers tightened on his.

"I am quite . . sure now we . . shall find . . Papa."

"I think the gods are on our side," the Marquis replied, "in fact, I am sure of it. I was thinking after you left me how fortunate we were to have reached Bangkok so quickly."

He paused and then went on:

"We then found the postcard which your father anticipated I would receive, if I asked for it in the right place."

"I should . . not have been . . so foolish," Ankana said humbly.

"As I have already said, it was understandable," the Marquis replied. "Actually if the thought upsets you, let me say I did not sample any of the 'delights' that are to be found in the place I visited."

He stopped speaking and smiled at her before adding:

"Instead I talked very seriously to the Proprietress."

He knew without being told that what he said pleased Ankana.

Because he was aware he had now set her mind at rest he said:

"Go to sleep. I want your father to see you looking pretty and happy when we find him, and not a woe-begone young woman with lines under her eyes and a red nose!"

"My nose is not red!" Ankana retorted, and the Marquis laughed.

"It is a very pretty, very attractive little nose! Now, as I am tired, I am going to bed, and I do not wish to be disturbed by strange noises coming from this cabin!"

"I . . I am sorry . . to have been . . so stupid."

"You were just being unpredictable," the Marquis replied, "and what woman is ever anything else. Good-night Ankana!"

He bent forward as he spoke, meaning to kiss her cheek.

She must have lifted her face to his and quite by accident he touched instead of her cheek, her lips.

For one moment he was held captive by the softness and innocence of them.

Then hastily, because he realised it was a mistake, he

rose to his feet saying as he did so:

"Sleep well, and perhaps tomorrow night your father will be with us."

He walked to the door, opened it, and went out without looking back.

Only as he reached his own cabin was he aware that he could still feel Ankana's lips.

He knew in some extraordinary way that kiss had been different from any kiss he had given or received in all his life.

Chapter Six

Ankana awoke very early, though she had not fallen asleep until hours after the Marquis had left her.

She had lain thinking of his kiss and feeling the touch of his lips on hers.

Because she had never been kissed, but already knew she loved him, it was an experience that seemed to ripple through her whole body like the waves of the sea.

She knew if he never touched her again she would always remember the feelings he had aroused in her.

It was a rapture of something she had never expected to happen.

It was everything she had longed for but never thought to find, certainly not with the Marquis of all people.

"How could I have ever hated him?" she asked herself.

She knew that he had intrigued and fascinated her from the first moment he had stopped being angry at her intrusion into his life.

He had treated her then as his guest, and as somebody whom he liked to talk to in an intelligent way.

She had never expected that anyone but her father would talk to her as to an equal, and would be so knowledgeable or, as she knew now, so exciting as a man.

She knew she had hated him for the life he led in London.

She despised the way she imagined he was wasting his brain and his capabilities in the Social World.

Now he was everything a man ought to be.

He was strong, authoritative and dignified, and at the same time gentle, understanding, and above all very exciting.

She was aware his kiss could mean nothing to him.

She knew however, for her it had opened a whole new horizon of wonders she had never considered before.

For the first time she thought of herself as a woman alone with a handsome and very fascinating man.

"Why could I not have discovered this earlier?" she asked.

She thought despairingly that their voyage was almost at an end.

Once they had found her father, the Marquis would doubtless return to England.

She could understand it was his duty to do so, as well being his real life.

She was intelligent enough to know it was only because he had shared adventures with her father before he came into his title that he felt he could not refuse the King of Siam's plea for help.

But that all belonged to the past.

Once the Marquis had rescued her father he would disappear like the mist over the sea.

It was doubtful if she would ever see him again.

"I love . . him!" she wispered.

Because it was impossible to sleep, she got out of bed and drawing back the curtains looked out of the port-hole.

They had steamed into the Bay of Pattaya so quietly that she had not been aware of it.

Now she could see a curving stretch of brilliant white sand, lapped by the waves, and behind it palm trees and bushes vivid with blossom.

It was so lovely that for a moment Ankana could only stare at it and feel she had stepped into some strange Paradise.

Hurriedly she began to dress, determined to see more of

what she thought was too beautiful a place for danger.

The Marquis had also lain awake for a long time.

He therefore did not get up, as he had intended, to see the '*Sea Horse*' move into the Bay of Pattaya.

He looked out through a port-hole on the other side of the yacht from Ankana's.

He saw a small tropical island surrounded by the darker blue of a coral-reef, the sea sparkling in the rising sun.

He too thought it was very beautiful, but as it was still very early he went back to bed.

He was thinking of Calvin Brook, and wondering if, now they were near him, Ankana would be able to get in touch with him by thought.

She had convinced him it was possible against his doubts and his logical mind.

Dobson called him at the usual time.

After he was dressed, looking exceedingly smart in his white trousers and blue yachting-jacket ornamented with gold buttons, he went up to the Saloon to have breakfast.

As a steward hurried in with a pot of coffee the Marquis asked:

"I see the table is laid only for one. Is Miss Ankana having breakfast in her cabin?"

"Miss Ankana's gone ashore, M'Lord."

"Ashore?"

The question was an exclamation both of surprise and apprehension.

"Yes, M'Lord. She asked some time ago for the boat to row her to the beach."

The Marquis hastily drank some of his coffee and rose to his feet.

A steward, realising his intention, hurriedly handed him his cap.

Putting it on, the Marquis quickly picked up a revolver from where they were stored behind the sofa.

He loaded it, and put it into his pocket.

Two seamen rowed him ashore, and he stepped out into the white sand.

He climbed a few low rocks, and ascended without difficulty the incline beyond them.

To his right there were cliffs forming the south end of the bay.

He was aware from the map that from there the coast curved round towards Chanthaburi and the Gem mines.

He thought probably the King had been right when he suggested that the thieves, whoever they might be, had come from that part of the country.

He could however be certain of nothing, except that it was a mistake for Ankana to have gone ashore without him.

He could understand that she had been beguiled by the beautiful, unspoiled view she could see from the yacht.

Of course, she was in a hurry to find her father.

At the other end of the bay there were a number of small fishing-boats at anchor and a few scattered houses.

No scene could have been quieter or more peaceful.

At the same time the Marquis was worried.

When he had climbed well above the beach, he looked ahead.

He saw that the ground to his right rose sharply to form a small hill covered with trees.

As he looked more closely he saw rising above the trees on the top of the hill the spire of what he guessed must be a Buddhist Temple.

It was what he might have expected, and ordinarily he would have dismissed it as being unimportant.

Now, however, as he looked at the spire shining in the sunshine, he had a strange feeling that he was drawn to it in a way he could not explain.

For a moment he hesitated.

It was unlikely that in her exploration of Pattaya, Ankana

would go straight to the Temple in search of her father.

Then once again his eyes were drawn to the pointed spire silhouetted against the blue of the sky.

Involuntarily his feet started to move in that direction.

It was a rough path twisting up the hillside.

The Marquis, who normally was very athletic, found himself enjoying the exercise.

He knew it was something he needed after being cooped up for so long in the '*Sea Horse*'.

He had walked as much as it was possible round and round the deck every day and had done exercises in his cabin.

Yet it was not the same as feeling his legs moving steadily over the dry ground with the freshness of the sea air on his face.

The sun was warm, but not too hot, there were birds singing in the trees, some of them exceedingly beautiful.

The fragrance of the blossoms and the pines combined with the salt in the air was very refreshing.

He would have enjoyed every moment, if he had not been pre-occupied with anxiety as to where Ankana had gone.

It seemed that, incredibly she had been so foolish as to think she could find her father by herself.

He had nearly reached the top of the hill when a twist in the path showed him the Temple which lay ahead.

It was small and old, and he was sure only used by the local labourers and fishermen.

It was of no interest to the small number of tourists who occasionally ventured as far from Bangkok as Pattaya.

The narrowness of the path, now little more than a track, was evidence of that.

The roof of the Temple which was open on two sides was badly in need of paint and repair.

There seemed to be no one about and the Marquis had stopped.

He was thinking that he would retrace his steps, when a sudden commotion broke out in the Temple.

Instinctively he ran towards it.

Ankana, like the Marquis, had seen the Temple as soon as she reached the higher ground above the beach.

She had been sending out her thoughts to her father from the moment she left the yacht.

She saw it over the palm trees moving slightly in the breeze and the rough grass interspersed with shrubs.

A hill rose sharply and unexpectedly from the level ground up to a peak.

As she looked at the spire of the Temple she felt she must pray for assistance.

Her father had taught her long ago that it was prayer that linked mankind with the Divine.

It was of no importance where on prayed, or in what particular faith, or to what god.

Because she understood what he had said to her, Ankana had prayed in Mosques and Cathedrals, in Temples and Chapels wherever they had travelled.

She found too, just as she could link herself in her thoughts with her father, that it was also possible to make contact with the Divine.

This applied especially when she was in need of help.

Now as she climbed up first the rough path, then the track which led to the Temple, she was concentrating her entire being on finding her father.

At the same time, she was praying for help and that she would not find him in danger.

She reached the Temple and saw it was very poor and badly in need of repair.

She found there were six steps that led up into it.

At the bottom of them there was a table on which there were small pieces of gold leaf for sale.

They were pressed for protection between pieces of

white paper and tied between two joss-sticks.

Because it was early in the morning there was no one in attendance at the table.

Ankana found a small coin in the pocket of her gown.

Taking the joss-sticks from a vase in which they were displayed, she climbed up the cracked steps into the Temple.

The roughly carved figure of a Buddha, cross-legged on a platform, was, she thought, very old.

It was covered almost completely by pieces of gold leaf.

In front of it the gold leaf on a huge foot flinted in the sunshine coming through an archway.

At first Ankana thought she was alone.

Then she saw in a corner of the Temple there was a monk wearing the orange robe of his calling.

He was kneeling as if in prayer his shaven head bowed so that she could see only the top of it.

She only gave him a glance, then carefully applied the gold leaf to the foot of Buddha.

She found it difficult to locate a place that was not already covered.

She lit her two joss-sticks and placed them in a tray of sand in front of the statue, lighting them from a small candle that was already burning.

Then with her palms pressed together in the correct gesture of prayer, she stood to one side looking up at the face of Buddha.

She was praying with a rapt intensity for her father.

Her eyes were shut and she was not aware that two men had entered the Temple from the opposite side to which she had come in herself.

She heard them move, but her brain did not register it.

Suddenly she heard a man shout.

As she opened her eyes, she saw to her astonishment a small man staggering backwards.

He had been struck by the monk who had been at prayer.

While he staggered, but did not actually fall, the other man turned on the monk.

They were striking each other violently with their fists.

To her utter astonishment Ankana realised that the monk who was fighting so ferociously was her father.

The man he was attacking was shorter than he was.

At the same time he was younger, and obviously accustomed to using his fists.

With a sense of horror Ankana saw the man her father had struck first, bring a knife from his clothing.

He moved towards him.

As he raised the knife, she realised that he was intending to drive it into her father's back.

It was then, in a flash of a second she picked up the tray of sand which held the candles and joss-sticks.

She threw it at the man with all her strength.

It took him by surprise.

As he fell back after the impact, and the sand flew into his face, blinding him, Ankana ran forward.

She was attempting to pull the knife from his hand.

He, however, recovered in time to stop her and putting his other arm round her neck he held her prisoner.

She cried out in fear and also because he was hurting her.

At that moment the Marquis ran into the Temple.

Seeing instantly what was happening he drew his revolver from his pocket and shot the man that Calvin Brook was fighting, in the leg.

At the sound of the explosion the other man, holding Ankana captive and still half-blinded by the sand in his eyes, raised his knife.

The Marquis with the experience of a crack-shot sent a bullet through his arm.

The man screamed, dropped the knife and released Ankana.

As he collapsed on the ground clutching his wounded

arm, Ankana ran to her father.

She flung her arms round his neck.

"Oh, Papa! Is it really you?"

Calvin Brook held her close to him while he looked at the Marquis.

"Thank you, Osmond," he said. "I might have guessed you would turn up in the nick of time!"

"I am glad we have found you, Calvin," the Marquis said quietly. "What are we to do about this offal?"

He looked contemptuously as he spoke at the two men who were lying on the floor, blood pouring from their wounds.

"Leave them," Calvin Brook said sharply, "and let us get out of here as quickly as possible!"

He moved Ankana to one side as he spoke, and to her surprise went towards the foot of the Buddha.

She thought now that was where the men must have been standing when her father first attacked them.

She saw him look down at the five toes covered with gold leaf.

Then he quickly picked up from each one of them a stone which she knew without being told, where the blue sapphires which he had been seeking.

They disappeared beneath his robe, and he beckoned to Ankana and the Marquis.

He led them through an arched opening on the opposite side of the Temple, through which the two men must have come.

Here there were six steps, as on the other side.

They led to a path twisting between the trees and so narrow that they could only move in single file.

After a short walk, descending a hill as steeply as by a ladder, they reached the ground.

They were above the cliffs which formed the end of the bay.

Still leading the way, Calvin Brook did not speak, and as if he had ordered silence, Ankana and the Marquis just followed him.

He moved very quickly.

Once they had reached flat ground they began to run towards the beach lying nearest to where the '*Sea Horse*' was anchored.

A boat manned by two seamen was beached on the sand waiting for them.

As soon as they appeared the two men began to ease the boat into the water.

They left just the stern on the sand for their three passengers to embark without getting their feet wet.

Once they were aboard, the seamen pushed the boat afloat, took up their oars, and rowed them swiftly towards the yacht.

Only as Calvin Brook looked back at the Temple spire which they could just see through the trees did Ankana say softly:

"I knew you were alive!"

"I thought you would," he answered simply.

They reached the yacht and climbed aboard without saying any more.

Only when they were alone in the Saloon, stewards having been sent to bring breakfast, did the Marquis say:

"I must say, Calvin, I find it hard to recognise you!"

"What was important," Calvin Brook replied, "was that nobody else should do so!"

"I really believed you to be a monk when I first entered the Temple," Ankana said.

"As it happens, I was sleeping," Calvin Brook said with a smile, "and I only awoke when those two ruffians arrived, and I realised to my horror that they were there."

"And Ankana had no right to be there either!" the Marquis reprimanded. "She crept out without telling me, and I was exceedingly alarmed that she might be in danger."

Ankana looked at him quickly, fearing he was angry.

Then she said softly:

"I . . I am sorry. I just wanted to . . look at the land because it seemed so attractive . . and then I thought I would . . say a prayer that we would . . find Papa."

"Your prayers were fortunately answered," Calvin Brook said, "and I too have been praying that Osmond would get my postcard and know where to find me."

"It was clever of you to send it to Beebe," the Marquis said.

"I was almost certain that the King would send for you when he received as I expected, a report of my death," Calvin Brook said, and paused a moment before he went on:

"I was only afraid you would be too grand or too busy to oblige His Majesty!"

Calvin's eyes were twinkling and there was laughter in his voice as he spoke.

"You should know me better than that!" the Marquis replied. "But I had no intention whatever of bringing Ankana with me. She was a stowaway, and I did not find her until we were in the Bay of Biscay."

Calvin Brook laughed.

"Ankana always gets her own way," he said, "as I expect you have found by now."

Ankana looked towards the Marquis a little nervously.

She wondered what his reply would be, but the stewards came into the Saloon at that moment.

They served their breakfast, and there was no chance to say any more.

Calvin Brook ate an enormous meal, saying he had had little to eat for days, and nothing at all for the last twenty-four hours.

After that he insisted on having a bath.

He also borrowed some of the Marquis's clothes before he would tell them what they were both very curious to learn.

Meanwhile the Marquis gave the order that the '*Sea Horse*' was to proceed immediately back to Bangkok.

When she was alone with him, Ankana asked surprisingly humbly:

"Are you . . angry with me?"

"I should have been not only very angry, but extremely distressed, if you had been in danger, even killed, as you well might have been."

"I suspect the truth is you would have been glad to be rid of an encumbrance," Ankana said lightly.

"I will answer that another time," the Marquis said. "At the moment I know that, like me, all you want to hear is the whole story of your father's exploits."

He paused a moment and then went on:

"I am sure you want to know as much as I do why he was forced to disguise himself very effectively as a Buddhist monk."

Ankana gave a little laugh as she said:

"You are lending him your clothes, but I suppose you have nothing so useful as a wig on board? He will certainly look strange until he can grow his hair."

"It may take some time, I suppose," the Marquis said, "but unless he wishes, which I think unlikely, to have many social engagements, it will not, I am sure, perturb him unduly."

They went out on deck to look at the coast-line they were passing on their way back to Bangkok.

But they were both finding it difficult to think of anything except what only Calvin Brook could tell them.

He came to join them dressed like the Marquis in yachting-clothes that were slightly too big for him.

In fact there was only his shaven head to make him look

anything but an English gentleman.

They sat down under the awning in a secluded part of the deck and as they did so the Marquis said:

"We are not going to ply you with questions. Start from the beginning and tell us everything that has happened."

"I expect the King told you," Calvin Brook began, "that I happened to be in Bangkok having a rest after returning from a very rough and uncomfortably dangerous part of Cambodia, which is another story."

He stopped speaking a moment, and then continued:

"I realised, as His Majesty did, that the finding of the sapphires was tremendously important."

"I am sure that His Majesty did not exaggerate the importance of them to the people of Chiang Mai," the Marquis remarked.

"No, indeed, and if they thought they had been stolen by a Burmese, it might have given rise to raids over the borders."

Calvin Brook stopped speaking, and looked at them both before he continued:

"These raids could easily have escalated into open warfare in which doubtless many lives would have been lost."

He paused before he went on:

"I was almost certain that the thieves were not Burmese but Cambodians."

He dropped his voice a little before saying:

"They were not only avaricious, but deeply resented that they had not been able to acquire the Gem district when other parts of Siamese land were ceded to her neighbours."

"I can understand that," the Marquis remarked quietly and Calvin Brook went on:

"With the Holy sapphires in their hands, it would be quite easy for them to start what would have been ostensibly a Holy War."

He stopped speaking and shook his head.

"Actually it would be a guerilla-like operation in which a great number of innocent people would lose their lives."

"But how did you know that the sapphires would be here?" Ankana asked because she could not control her curiosity any longer.

"First I must tell you what happened in Chiang Mai," her father replied. "Thanks to the King's quickness and help, I was there three days after the theft."

He stopped speaking and smiled at them.

"I then discovered that the Abbot of the Temple from which they had been taken had been extremely astute."

He paused before he went on:

"He notified the Police secretly that a theft had occurred of all the gold ornaments that surrounded the sacred image of the Buddha."

Ankana looked puzzled, and her father explained:

"On the Abbot's insistence, the Police then scrutinised and searched everybody leaving Chiang Mai."

"Oh . . I see!" Ankana said. "So you thought the sapphires had not yet left the City."

"If, as I thought, they planned to take them to Cambodia," her father answered, "they would have to proceed down the river by boat to Bangkok, where they would have boarded a larger vessel to carry them down the Gulf of Siam."

Ankana was listening with her large eyes fixed on her father's face.

The Marquis watching her thought she looked very lovely.

He supposed, now that her father was here to chaperon her, there was no more need for her to pretend to be so young, and to wear her hair loose over her shoulders.

He had a sudden, almost irresistible desire to touch it before she could arrange it fashionably on top of her head.

Then surprised at his own feelings, the Marquis forced

himself to listen to what Calvin Brook was saying.

"As I expected," Calvin replied, "it was impossible for the thieves to pass out of the walled City without being searched. Moreover they had to wait for a boat to take them down the river."

He paused a moment and then continued:

"It was essential that they should move at night. Somehow I do not know how it happened, in the dark I became separated from the two Policemen who were working with me.

"Then I was suddenly aware that just ahead of me there were three men, two of them already getting into a boat that had been concealed in the foliage on the bank of the river.

"I rushed forward to tackle the last man who was still standing on the bank.

"While I did so the two men in the boat ordered the oarsmen to pull away and they set off downstream, quite unperturbed that their confederate had been left behind!

"He fought me vigorously, determined, I am sure, to kill me, so that he could swim after the others and get his share of the spoils they carried."

"He might have . . killed you . . Papa!" Ankana said in a frightened voice.

"That is what I thought," her father answered, "but as it was a question of my life or his, I decided he was the more dispensable!"

Ankana moved a little closer to her father as he went on:

"It was only after I had killed him that I realised since his confederates had seen me very clearly in the moonlight, that I was a marked man!"

"So that is why you pretended to die!" Ankana exclaimed.

"I fortunately had some papers with me – not important ones – and I wrote my name on them before I planted them in the man's pocket."

He paused, and had a wry smile on his face before he went on:

"Then to make certain there would be no mistake, I slipped my signet-ring onto his finger."

"That was clever of you," the Marquis said.

"Common sense!" Calvin Brook smiled. "I then put him face downwards in the rushes, knowing that by the time the body was found his face would be unrecognisable. Then I disappeared."

"Was that not difficult? Surely the Police were looking for you?"

"I have 'disappeared' a great many times before," Calvin Brook smiled, "as Osmond well knows."

"Go on," the Marquis said.

"The next thing I had to do was to find out exactly where the thieves were going. By good fortune, the boat for Cambodia they had expected to join in Bangkok had left the day before they arrived."

Ankana made a little sound of excitement but she did not interrupt.

"It was then I think they panicked, being afraid somebody would inform on them if they stayed in the City. They therefore boarded a fishing-boat that was going down river, then out to sea."

"So that is how they landed up in Pattaya," the Marquis remarked.

"Exactly!" Calvin Brook replied. "And while they were waiting there, they cleverly hid the sapphires in the Temple above the bay."

"How did you learn that?" Ankana asked breathlessly.

"By the time I got to Bangkok," her father replied, "I had already disguised myself as a Buddhist monk. Because they are reverred in this country everybody treated me with courtesy."

He stopped speaking a moment then went on:

"I could ask questions that might have seemed suspicious or too revealing had I not been enveloped with an aura of holiness."

He looked across at the Marquis as he said:

"As you well know, Osmond, we have friends, or at least confederates, in very strange places!"

"You do!" the Marquis replied pointedly.

"With a little encouragement, and of course because I am in a privileged position, they told me that two men, who had wanted urgently to get to Cambodia, had had to be content with being taken by a well-known fisherman only as far as Pattaya."

"And why did you think the stones would be in the Temple?" Ankana asked.

"Because they are so valuable, I thought it was unlikely that the men would walk about with them in their pockets, since they might by accident get into a fight of have other thieves searching them for money while they slept."

"And what made you think they would take their spoils to the Temple?"

"Where else?" Calvin Brook asked. "It is very unusual as you well know, in this country for anyone to risk being cursed or, at the very least, incurring a great deal of bad luck, if they rob the Lord Buddha himself!"

"So you went to the Temple!" Ankana exclaimed.

"I went to the Temple to wait for them to arrive. But of course I had no idea where in that rather ramshackle building they had hidden the stones."

His voice dropped slightly as he went on:

"It might have been in the earth, under the statue itself, or more daringly on the toes of the Buddha's foot from where they had extracted them in Chiang Mai."

"It was very brave of you, Papa, to go it all alone."

"I had no idea who else I could trust," her father replied, "and I thought I could manage the two of them on my own. I am only grateful that Osmond arrived, exactly as I had hoped he would, at the very moment he was wanted!"

"My advice is not to push your luck!" the Marquis said. "If Ankana had not been here to distract the man who was about to knife you in the back, we might have had a very different story to tell."

"I know," Calvin Brook replied, "and I am extremely grateful to be alive."

He looked at his daughter very lovingly as he said:

"Thank you my poppet. At the same time, although I could feel your thoughts winging towards me, I imagined you were in London, attending Balls and making your curtsy at Buckingham Palace."

"That is what the Marquis wanted me to do," Ankana replied, "but I knew you were in danger, Papa, and I could hardly listen to the inane conversation of the young men who danced with me when I was terrified that you might be dead!"

Calvin Brook kissed her forehead before he said:

"What is the use of my arranging for you to be a Society Lady if you run away to risk your life among thieves and cut-throats?"

"You can hardly complain I am doing that," Ankana protested, "when I have spent three weeks in the company of a real live Marquis!"

She gave the Marquis a provocative glance, and he said:

"You will understand that once Ankana was aboard, short of chucking her to the fishes, the only thing I could do was to put up with her and for convention's sake pretend that she was much younger than she really is."

"I wondered why her hair was down," Calvin Brook remarked. "You must now go back immediately to your aunt and try to behave as a Lady should."

He appeared to be speaking seriously, though his eyes were twinkling and Ankana gave a cry of horror before she protested:

"No, Papa, no! I cannot go through that all over again. I want to be with you!"

"I am afraid that is impossible."

"Why?" Ankana asked.

"Because I have promised," he answered, "and actually it is something I very much want to do."

He stopped speaking to smile at her before he went on:

"I want to visit Tibet in search of some very special manuscripts which are said to be in one of the Monasteries. It will mean my staying with the monks for several months, if not longer."

He pulled her a little closer as he said:

"However much you plead with me, my lovely daughter, you will understand that there is no possible way I can take you with me, for it is certain the monks would not open their doors to a young woman."

"That is certainly true," the Marquis remarked.

Ankana got up from the sofa on which she was sitting beside her father and walked to the window of the Saloon.

They were moving quickly through the calm sea and she thought it would not be long before they reached the entrance to the *Menam Chao Phya*.

She knew that, once they were in Bangkok and her father had handed the sapphires over to the King, it was doubtful if he would be with them for very much longer.

She knew him so well that she recognised the note of excitement in his voice when he spoke of going to Tibet.

She remembered it was something he had always wanted to do.

Now that he had the opportunity, nothing would dissuade him from leaving as quickly as possible.

That meant that she must rely on the Marquis to take her back with him to England.

Unless of course, he had other plans.

In which case she would be put in charge of some respectable lady and sent back on the first ship that called at Bangkok on the homeward voyage.

As she moved away she was debating with herself whether she should plead with the Marquis to let her sail back with him on the '*Sea Horse*'.

He was not looking at her, but at her father, as he said:

"It sounds extremely interesting, Calvin, although I dare say you will find it somewhat uncomfortable."

"That does not worry me," Calvin Brook replied. "I have managed to obtain an invitation to the most important Monastery in Tibet, and the promise that I shall be received by the Dali Lama."

There was a note of satisfaction in the way he spoke which told both the Marquis and Ankana that to him it was a dream come true.

After a moment the Marquis said:

"I wish I could come with you."

"There is nothing I would enjoy more," Calvin Brook replied.

Ankana drew in her breath.

Then she could not bear to know that she was not only to lose her father but also the Marquis.

They were the two men who mattered most in her life!

She turned and without any explanation went out of the Saloon slamming the door behind her.

As Calvin Brook looked after her in surprise, the Marquis said:

"I want to talk to you about Ankana."

Chapter Seven

The Marquis went down the companionway and along the passage to Ankana's cabin.

He paused outside the door, then without knocking walked in.

As he did so Ankana jumped off the bed and ran to the port-hole.

The Marquis shut the door behind him without speaking.

Ankana asked:

"Is that you, Papa?"

There was a little sob in her voice and the Marquis walked slowly across the cabin until he stood beside her.

Then he asked gently:

"Why are you crying?"

"I am not!" she answered defiantly like a child.

But he could see the tears running down her cheeks, and after a moment he said:

"I know it has upset you that your father is going away so quickly!"

She gave a little gasp.

"What . . what is . . Papa doing?"

She spoke frantically and the Marquis replied:

"He said he wanted to rest and when I left him lying on a sofa in the Saloon he was already asleep."

He knew she gave a little sigh of relief and he went on:

"Your father was able to sleep very little while he was waiting in the Temple for the thieves, but now he is determined, and I think it wise to leave on the first ship from Bangkok which calls at Calcutta."

He paused a moment, and then went on:

"Then he will start his journey to Tibet."

He saw Ankana clasp her hands together as if she forced herself not to cry out.

After a moment she asked in a hestitating little voice:

"A.are you . . going with . . him?"

The Marquis shook his head.

"I have other plans, which I want to discuss with you."

Ankana was certain he was going to tell her that he was making arrangements for her return to England.

Because she felt she could not bear to hear him actually say the words she turned her head away, saying a little incoherently:

"Must we . . discuss it . . n.now?"

"I think you may be interested," the Marquis replied, "as I am planning my honeymoon."

Ankana stiffened, then in a voice he could hardly recognise she asked:

"D.did you . . s.say . . your h.honeymoon?"

"I think it would be the solution of your problems as well as mine."

Now she turned to stare at him, her eyes with their wet eye-lashes very large in her small face.

"W.what are you . . saying? I . . I do not . . understand!"

The Marquis smiled, then slowly, as if he forced himself not to hurry, he put his arms around her and drew her close to him.

"What has happened to your perception and the ability you claim to read thoughts," he asked, "if you do not know already that I love you?"

"It . . it cannot be . . true!" Ankana whispered.

"It is true," the Marquis said. "I have been in love with you for a very long time."

He stopped speaking to look at her, before he went on:

"When I saw that man raise his knife to stab you, I knew that if I lost you I should have lost everything that was precious and my life would never be the same again."

He did not wait for her answer, but held her closer still and his lips held hers captive.

To Ankana it was as if the whole world had vanished and she was flying in the sky.

The feelings she had known for the first time when the Marquis had touched her lips before, now seemed to intensify.

They became so thrilling that they seeped through her and she quivered with the ecstasy of them.

It was what she had dreamed true love would be like.

She had known she would never find in the Social World into which her father had sent her, and where her aunt was determined she would find a husband.

Now as the Marquis held her closer and closer still and his kiss became more demanding, more possessive, she knew he was everything she wanted in a man.

Her love for him was as deep as the sea, as high as the sky.

It came from the Power in which both she and her father believed.

It was so perfect, so like touching the Divine, that the tears ran again down her cheeks.

When the Marquis raised his head he said in a voice that was deep and moved:

"You are not crying, my precious?"

"Only . . because I am so . . happy! I love you . . but I never . . thought you would . . love me!"

"It will take a long time to tell you how much," the Marquis said, "and that is why we will have a very long honeymoon."

As if he could not wait for her answer, he kissed her again.

As her body seemed to melt into his, he knew that no woman had ever made him feel as he was feeling at this moment.

"What have you done to me, my darling," he asked a little later, "to make me feel like this?"

"How . . do you feel?" Ankana asked, her eyes shining like stars.

"I feel as if I have conquered the world, found what I have always been seeking, the Golden Fleece and the Holy Grail and now my pilgrimage is over."

"Are you . . sure of that . . absolutely . . sure?"

"It is something I have to prove, but when we celebrate our Golden Wedding, you will be able to tell me I was right!"

Ankana gave a little laugh. Then she said:

"If we are . . going to be married . . please . . can I have a new gown? I was only able to bring two muslin ones with me when I crept aboard . . and they are now . . almost in rags!"

The Marquis laughed.

"I think, my darling," he said, "this is the first time I have heard you being really feminine! I never thought of it before, but of course we have been at sea for a long time."

He smiled at her and then went on:

"I am sure your wardrobe which you had to carry yourself cannot have been very extensive."

"I thought it did . . not matter, as you were not . . at all . . interested in . . me," Ankana explained, "but now I want to look . . pretty for . . you."

"You look beautiful!" the Marquis said. "And I adore you with your hair down as you are wearing it at this moment."

He stopped speaking a moment and then carried on:

"I suppose people will be somewhat surprised if my wife looks like a little girl, so we will buy some gowns quickly in Bangkok."

He kissed her eyes before he went on:

"Then we will spend part of our honeymoon in Hong Kong, where the Chinese shop-keepers will provide you with everything you need."

He paused before he added:

"With their talent for copying everything one requires within twenty-four hours, you will soon be able to fill every wardrobe and cupboard there is on board!"

Ankana laughed at this. Then she said:

"I am not greedy . . but I am . . afraid if I look too . . disreputable you might stop . . loving me."

"That is impossible!"

The Marquis knew as he spoke that he did not love Ankana as he had loved other women, simply because she was beautiful.

Spiritually and mentally they were linked in a very different way from anything he had ever known before.

"I love your clever little brain," he said, "and one thing is quite certain – with you I shall never be bored or cynical."

Ankana gave a little cry.

"Now you are . . frightening . . me!"

"On the contrary, I am reassuring you," the Marquis answered. "I was thinking only this morning that I know of no other woman with whom I could have spent so long a time, completely alone, and never known one minute's boredom!"

"Is that really true?" Ankana asked.

"I swear to you that it is!" the Marquis answered. "Every night when you sent me to bed thinking of you, going over what we had discussed and argued about, you stimulated my mind until I found it hard not to come to your cabin and go on talking to you."

His arms tightened as he said:

"In future there will be no problems about talking to you, but I expect the subject, my precious, will be of love."

He felt Ankana quiver and thought it was the most

exciting thing he had ever known.

Then he was kissing her again; kissing her until it was impossible to think or talk, or do anything but feel.

Later, when Calvin Brook was awake, they went to the Saloon hand-in-hand to tell him the good news.

"I cannot imagine anything which could give me more satisfaction!" he said. "I have always been frightened, my darling daughter, that the man you married would not be worthy of you."

He smiled and went on:

"I know Osmond so well, and we have been together in so many strange places and even thought we might die together side-by-side, that I can imagine no one whom I would rather have as a son-in-law."

"Thank you, Calvin!" the Marquis said with a smile.

"I know you will look after Ankana," Calvin Brook went on. "At the same time, I have always found her not only an entrancing companion, but somebody who has inspired me and given me ambitions I never had before."

"That is something I have already discovered," the Marquis said quietly.

"Now you are both making me feel . . embarrassed," Ankana protested, "and, please, Papa . . do not be away for . . too long."

"I will certainly be back in time to see my first grandchild!" Calvin Brook replied.

The Marquis thought the blush which made Ankana look shy was very lovely.

When the '*Sea Horse*' reached Bangkok, Dobson was sent hurrying to the best and most expensive dressmakers.

He told them to bring their gowns to the yacht for Ankana to choose what she required.

While she was doing this, the Marquis and her father went to the Palace to give the King the five sapphires and to tell him their mission was accomplished.

The King was, as they expected, delighted. At the same time he said seriously:

"I think, Mr. Brook, it would be a great mistake for you to linger here in Bangkok, and the same applies to you, My Lord."

He gave a deep sigh before he continued:

"The hostile elements in Cambodia can be very unpleasant, especially when any of their number are killed or wounded."

"We are aware of that, Your Majesty," Calvin Brook said. "In fact, I am leaving tonight in a ship which will carry me to Calcutta."

He stopped speaking a moment and then continued:

"You may be interested to know that I shall be travelling under an assumed name, so that it will be difficult for any who seek revenge to find me."

"That is sensible," the King approved, "and you know anything you require that I can provide is at your disposal."

"I thank Your Majesty."

The King looked at the Marquis who said:

"I also have planned, Your Majesty, to leave Bangkok this evening, but before I do so, I intend to be married at the Anglican Episcopal Church to Ankana Brook!"

"That is excellent news!" the King exclaimed. "Excellent! I thought her a very charming, very beautiful young lady, and I feel sure, My Lord, you will be very happy."

"I am quite certain of that!" the Marquis replied. "But your Majesty will understand that you will be the only person who will know about our marriage."

The King looked gratified and the Marquis continued:

"For the same reason that Mr. Brook is travelling under an assumed name, I shall be married quietly under my family name without my title, and intend there should be no observers and certainly no interested representatives of the press."

The King thought for a moment, before he said:
"I have a better idea than that! I think it would be a mistake for you to move about the City."
He stopped speaking and looked hard at the Marquis before continuing:
"Mr. Brook as we well know, is a master of disguise, but you My Lord, are too tall, too distinguished, and far too handsome to remain unnoticed."
The Marquis laughed a little ruefully as the King went on:
"I am aware that Missionaries in my country and in other parts of the world travel with a Consecrated Stone so that they can perform the Services of your Church . . even though the places in which those Services are held may sometimes be strange ones."
The Marquis was listening intently, knowing that what the King was saying was true.
He remembered, although he had not thought of it, that Missionaries in Africa always carried a Consecrated Stone.
Any table or rock on which they placed it became an altar.
"What I am going to suggest," the King went on, "is that instead of being married in your Church in the City, where you may be seen because a wedding always invites interest, you marry here in the Palace."
The Marquis looked surprised.
"As it happens, I learnt this morning that we have a visitor, a highly respected man who has been travelling in the North of my country, and has attended medically to many of our people who were struck down by a serious outbreak of typhoid."
Calvin Brook knew of whom he was speaking and murmured:
"Father Trevor Sutherland!"
"The same, and a very remarkable man!" the King affirmed. "As I wished to thank him personally for his

medical aid so affected, I have invited him here to the Palace as my guest."

There was no need to say any more, the Marquis thanked the King for his kindness.

The King promised to arrange that a room in the Palace of Calm Delights would be at their disposal by the time the Marquis wanted it.

When they returned to tell Ankana what had been arranged, they found her excited about the lovely gowns which had been brought to her on the yacht.

She had been very careful not to say that one of them was for her wedding.

Because she looked so young, the dressmakers expected her to be dressed in white and pale colours.

There was therefore, no suspicion that she required a white gown for any special reason.

She came into the Saloon wearing a simple white gown, made of an exquisite silk material.

Her hair was piled on top of her small head and caught with a wreath of flowers, and the Marquis realised she was no longer the young schoolgirl she had pretended to be, but very much a woman.

There was no question of her wearing a wedding-veil.

But the wreath of real flowers, was echoed in the bouquet the Marquis bought for her, made Ankana feel very bridal.

The King had sent one of the Royal carriages to carry them to the Palace of Calm Delights.

There they were met only by the Chamberlain who showed them into a room where Father Sutherland was waiting for them.

He had obviously taken his instructions from the King, and a table had been set up at the far end of the room.

It was covered with an exquisitely embroidered cloth of gold and silver thread.

There were six lighted candles standing on it in elaborate

holders of gold ornamented with precious stones.

In the centre of this unusual and exotic altar lay the Consecrated Stone with which Father Sutherland travelled.

There were huge vases of flowers that scented the room on either side of the Altar.

Garlands of flowers also decorated the pictures and the top of the windows and doors.

Ankana thought that no bride could have had a stranger but more attractive background for her wedding ceremony.

The Marquis and her father both wore evening-dress.

If by any chance they were seen, people would think they were merely going to dine with His Majesty at the Palace.

Father Sutherland read the Marriage Service with a sincerity that made every word very moving.

As Ankana knelt before him holding very tightly onto the Marquis's hand, she prayed that their love would be blessed.

She asked God to make her the sort of wife he wanted, even if his position in England produced many difficulties and problems for her.

She loved him so overwhelmingly that she knew whatever he asked of her she would do willingly.

At the same time she was intelligent enough to realise that her life in the future would be very different.

During the adventures she had enjoyed with her father, she had met so many strange but interesting people who had been their friends.

They would certainly not be accepted in the Social Life that she was entering as the Marquis's wife.

Just for a moment she was afraid that she could fail him and he might in consequence regret marrying her.

Then she told herself that the Power which had helped her to find her father was still with her.

It had carried her through dangers which would have

disconcerted or destroyed other women and it would not fail her now.

"Help me . . help me . . God!" she prayed in her heart.

She felt the Marquis's fingers tighten on hers and knew he was aware what she was thinking.

It seemed incredible that she had been fortunate enough to find a man, who where she was concerned, was almost as perceptive as her father.

She was sure that because they were so close to each other and would be closer still now that they were married, the Marquis's perception and instinct would further develop.

They would soon be one, not only with their bodies, but with their minds.

Father Sutherland blessed them.

As they rose and walked to the door of the Palace they saw that there were two of the Royal carriages waiting for them.

The Chamberlain who was waiting explained that His Majesty wanted a last word with Mr. Brook, who would follow them to the yacht in the second carriage.

Ankana and the Marquis therefore drove away alone.

Lifting her hand he kissed her fingers, one after the other.

"I find it . . hard to . . believe that I am . . really married to . . you," Ankana whispered in a shy little voice.

"You are my wife," the Marquis said, "and, darling, we have so many things to do together that I promise that in the future you need never be jealous of me again."

Ankana moved to lay her cheek against his shoulder as she asked:

"Did you . . realise that I was . . jealous?"

"It was then that I thought perhaps you loved me a little."

"I love you with my whole . . heart!" she answered.

"And now you fill not . . only my heart . . but my . . life!"

"That is what I wanted you to say."

He kissed her hand again.

When they arrived at the yacht, he helped her to alight, and they were waiting in the Saloon when Calvin Brook returned.

The Marquis waited curiously to learn why the King had wanted to see him.

Calvin Brook laughed.

"There is no need to ask what I know you are thinking," he said. "His Majesty unexpectedly had a small task for me to perform for him in Tibet which will be of benefit to Siam!"

The Marquis smiled.

"I guessed he would be anxious to keep in touch with you. You have done so much for this country that they will never let you go."

"I might do worse than settle here when I am too old to go adventuring!" Calvin Brook said. "It is the 'Land of Smiles' and I am always very happy with the Siamese."

"That is a lovely idea!" Ankana enthused. "And we will come to stay with you every year, so if you do settle here, be sure to buy a large house."

"I will do that!" her father promised.

He stayed for another hour and they had dinner together.

Then he drove away to where the ship which was to carry him to India was moored further down the river.

"Promise that you will take care of yourself!" Ankana begged. "I cannot go through the . . agony of hearing you are . . dead all over again!"

"You will know when I am," Calvin Brook said confidently. "In the meantime, whether I am in Tibet or on the moon, I will keep in touch with you, my darling."

"Please do that and I shall be praying for you."

"Your prayers will keep me safe, as they have done up to now," her father answered.

He drove away.

The Marquis knew that, while he was sad to be leaving Ankana, he was already excited by the adventure that lay ahead and the idea of staying in a Tibetan Monastery.

There was also the privilege of being allowed to inspect the priceless manuscripts which had been stored there for centuries.

When he had gone, the Marquis put his arm round Ankana.

He drew her down the companionway towards their cabins.

Without releasing her he opened his door and Ankana gave a little gasp.

While they had been at dinner, Dobson had changed the cabins over.

Now her clothes were in the cabin that had been the Marquis's, and it was filled with a profusion of flowers.

Only Dobson had known of their impending marriage.

Because it had to be kept so secret, not even the Captain had been aware of what was happening.

As the engines of the yacht were throbbing beneath them, they were moving slowly from their anchorage opposite the Palace down stream.

Ankana looked around at the flowers and then at one of the new nightgowns she had chosen earlier in the day and which was now lying on the bed.

Then she said involuntarily:

"I must not turn you out of your cabin, darling."

"*Our* cabin!" the Marquis corrected. "Have you forgotten, my precious little wife, that we are married!"

He put his hand under her chin and turned her face up to his.

"I could not kiss you," he said a little hoarsely, "until your father had left, because if I had done so, I would have found it hard to think of anything else."

His voice went deeper as he carried on:

"But now we are alone and you are mine, my darling, until the seas run dry and stars fall from the sky."

It was then he kissed her, holding her against him.

He thought the softness and sweetness of her was symbolic of what she would be to him as his wife.

He knew that he wanted her to be very feminine as a woman and to need his protection.

While at the same time she stimulated and inspired him in a way he had never been inspired before.

As his arms tightened around her he thought he was the most fortunate man in the world.

He had found so much in one small person that would intrigue, fascinate, and hold him captive for the rest of their lives.

A long time later the '*Sea Horse*' was anchored down river where no one would notice her and there were only the palm trees and the mango-groves on one side of it.

Ankana turned her face against her husband's shoulder and kissed it.

"I . . love you!" she whispered.

"What I feel for you is totally inexpressible," he said. "I have never, and this is the truth, my precious one, experienced such happiness as you have given me."

"Is that . . true . . really true?" Ankana asked. "I have been so . . afraid I might . . disappoint you."

"That is impossible," the Marquis said. "I did not know that anybody could be so beautiful, but you have given me so much more than that."

She moved a little closer to him and he went on:

"We are now one person, and as we think together, I feel that in some way we shall be more effective in what we can do to help other people, than if we acted singly."

"That is what I think too," Ankana said. "Oh, darling, I

know you are very important, but you promise me you will let . . me help . . you?"

"I know I can do nothing without you," the Marquis said. "It is a feeling I know will grow and grow in the future, and of course, we must bring up our children to be perceptive, as we are."

Ankana raised her face to his.

"I am praying I may . . give you a . . son," she whispered.

She knew that her words moved the Marquis for he said:

"I want children to fill the big house that is waiting for us at home, and who will carry on the family name."

He paused a moment, to smile at her before he went on:

"But I shall be jealous if you love them more than you love me, because I want your love more than I have ever wanted anything in my whole life."

"It is . . yours!" Ankana said quickly. "And I am . . yours . . too!"

"I have already said that I adore your beautiful and unusual face," the Marquis said.

He kissed her eyes as he spoke, her small straight nose, and the dimples on either side of her mouth before he went on:

"But I also find your brain entrancing, exciting, stimulating, and very original."

He stopped speaking to look intently at her, then added:

"One thing is certain – I know I shall never be bored by knowing exactly what you will say before you say it!"

Ankana laughed.

"That is a challenge, and if I am unpredictable and you find me exasperating, it will be your fault!"

"I will risk it!" the Marquis said.

He remembered how often he had been bored with other women because there was nothing original or unexpected about them.

Holding her a little closer, his hand moving over the

softness of her body, he went on:

"I love your heart which I think belongs to me as mine belongs to you, but there is something else, my sweet, which I have never asked of another woman, but which I want from you."

Ankana wrinkled her forehead to show she was mystified and the Marquis said very softly:

"I want your soul, the soul which makes you what you are, and which I know speaks to the Power which helps you, and which I want in my life too."

"It is yours! Everything . . that is . . mine is . . yours!" Ankana said.

There was a note of passion in her voice which the Marquis did not miss.

He had been very gentle and controlled in his love-making because he knew that the feelings he evoked in Ankana were different from anything she had experienced before.

She was like a blossom opening out to the sun, he knew he must not hurt or frighten her in any way.

Now he knew that he would teach her to love him as passionately as he loved her.

At the same time spiritually she had much to teach him.

He moved a little sideways so that he could look down at her.

"How can you be so perfect?" he asked. "How can you be the woman that has always been in a special shrine in my imagination, but whom I thought I would never find?"

"Are you . . quite, quite certain that now you have . . found me and know me . . you will not be . . bored?"

She was speaking half-teasingly, and yet there was a seriousness behind the words which the Marquis did not miss.

"I will answer that question," he said, "when we reach eternity together."

Then he was kissing her; kissing her demandingly, possessively.

Yet she was in herself as holy as the blue sapphire stones which were of such importance to the peace and happiness of Siam.

Then he felt Ankana's lips respond to his.

He was aware that the passion burning within him had lit a little flame within her.

She was responding so that the petals of the flower opened further and the Marquis felt a light from the Divine encircled them and came too from their souls.

"I love you! I love . . you!" Ankana whispered. "Please . . love me and . . make me . . yours!"

"You *are* mine!" the Marquis answered. "And I worship and adore you!"

They moved even closer to each other.

Then as the Marquis made Ankana his there was only the blazing light that came from Heaven itself.

And there was the soft lap of the Menam river against the yacht.

It was very early the next morning that Ankana awoke and because she was so happy she slipped out of the bed.

The Marquis was sleeping peacefully.

She knew as she could see him in the light coming through the port-holes that he looked younger and even more handsome than he had the previous day.

She had an impulse to go from there to the dressing-table to see if she too was transformed by love.

Instead she very quietly pulled back the curtains from the port-hole and looked out.

The sun had not yet risen but there was a golden glow in the sky.

The river through which they were moving had a faint mist over it which gave it an ethereal look which Ankana felt was typical of the whole country.

She knew that soon they would have left Siam behind and would be moving up the South China Sea towards Hong Kong.

Almost as if she was looking at a map she could visualise the world that they were approaching.

She knew that with her husband it would be a fascinating experience that would enthrall them both.

Last night the Marquis had aroused sensations and emotions within her that she never knew anybody could feel and still be alive on this earth.

In her mind she knew that he was right in saying they came from her soul.

The Divine Light was the physical and spiritual love which all men seek, but so seldom find.

It was the love that had made artists create great pictures, musicians compose music which lifted those who heard it into the spheres.

It was what the poets tried to express and sometimes succeeded.

"It is love . . real love!" Ankana said to herself.

Then she thought with a little shiver that she might have married one of the men her aunt had determined she should meet.

Then she would never have known the ecstasy she felt now or been aware of what she was missing.

"Thank You, thank You, God!" she said to the sun.

She knew that the God to whom she prayed was also Buddha whom she would never forget.

She was so intent on her thoughts that she started when the Marquis said from the bed:

"Why have you left me, my darling?"

She turned and ran back to throw herself down beside him.

As his arms went round her she looked up at him with shining eyes.

"I was thinking how . . fortunate I am to have . . found you," she answered.

"I was dreaming the same thing."

"I am so . . happy that I am . . afraid," Ankana whispered.

"Afraid?" the Marquis questioned.

"It is . . too perfect . . too wonderful to last . . I shall wake up to find that both you and the yacht have . . disappeared."

"You are not to be so imaginative!" the Marquis ordered. "I must teach you, my lovely one, to trust me so that never again will you be unsure of my love, or that you belong to me!"

Ankana moved a little closer to him.

"There are so many things for us to do together," she said softly, "but what is more exciting than anything else is that we think together, and when I am . . close to you like this . . everything else is of no importance."

The Marquis did not answer, and after a moment she went on:

"You are very grand and very rich . . but neither of those things matter . . and I should love just as much if we had to live in a tent or a cave . . and I could never again afford a new gown!"

The Marquis laughed.

"I expect if you were honest, when the time came, you would find it rather frustrating. But I understand what you are saying, my precious love, and I feel just the same."

He paused a moment and then went on:

"At the same time it is satisfying to know that we can afford to be comfortable, and there are so many expensive presents I would love to give you when eventually we return to England."

He realised that Ankana was wondering what these could be and he said:

"Chief among them are horses. Your father has told me

that you are an accomplished rider, but I have never seen you on a horse."

He stopped speaking to smile at her before saying:

"I have a feeling however that we shall ride well together, as we do everything else."

"I can think of no more exciting present you could give me than the sort of magnificent horse which I know you ride," Ankana cried.

The Marquis's lips touched her forehead as he said:

"Stop worrying about the future! You will not find the Balls, the Receptions or Buckingham Palace frightening when we are there together."

He kissed her little nose.

"We can laugh at those who take such things seriously, and slip away on our own where, as you have just said, we will be quite content in a tent or a cave."

Ankana gave a little cry.

"You understand! Oh, darling Osmond, you understand and that is the only thing that really matters!"

"What matters to me at the moment," the Marquis said, "is that I find you very alluring, very exciting, and I am not concerned with the future, but with my honeymoon!"

"How can I make it . . very . . special and . . something that you will always . . remember?" Ankana asked.

"Like this!" the Marquis replied.

Then he was kissing her, kissing her possessively until he felt her respond.

His lips became fiercer and more demanding.

For the first time there was a wildness in Ankana. A response in the beating of her heart.

"I love . . you . . I love . . you," she cried.

"Give me yourself," the Marquis pleaded. "I want you completely and utterly to be mine!"

"I am . . yours . . yours . . with all my heart . . and my Soul."

"And your body," the Marquis asked, "your lovely, soft, entrancing little body?"

"It is yours . . Oh, darling . . love me. I want . . to be yours . . all yours . . completely."

Then as the sun came through the port-hole enveloping them with its golden rays the Marquis carried Ankana into the burning heat of it.

OTHER BOOKS BY BARBARA CARTLAND

Romantic Novels, over 400, the most recently published being:
Crowned with Love
Escape
The Devil Defeated
The Secret of the Mosque
A Dream in Spain
The Love Trap
Listen to Love
The Golden Cage
Love Casts Out Fear
A World of Love
Dancing on a Rainbow
Love Joins the Clan
An Angel Runs Away
Forced to Marry
Bewildered in Berlin
Wanted – A Wedding Ring
The Earl Escapes
Starlight Over Tunis
The Love Puzzle
Love and Kisses
The Dream and the Glory
(In aid of the St. John Ambulance Brigade)

Autobiographical and Biographical:
The Isthmus Years 1919-1939
The Years of Opportunity 1939-1945
I Search for Rainbows 1945-1976
We Danced All Night 1919-1929
Ronald Cartland (With a foreword by Sir Winston Churchill)
Polly – My Wonderful Mother
I Seek the Maraculous

Historical:
Bewitching Women

The Outrageous Queen
(The Story of Queen Christina of Sweden)
The Scandalous Life of King Carol
The Private Life of Charles II
The Private Life of Elizabeth, Empress of Austria
Josephine, Empress of France
Diane de Poitiers
Metternich – The Passionate Diplomat

Sociology:
You in the Home
The Fascinating Forties
Marriage for Moderns
Be Vivid, Be Vital
Love, Life and Sex
Vitamins for Vitality
Husbands and Wives
Men are Wonderful
Etiquette
The Many Facets of Love
Sex and the Teenager
The Book of Charm
Living Together
The Youth Secret
The Magic of Honey
The Book of Beauty and Health
Keep Young and Beautiful by Barbara Cartland and Elinor Glyn
Etiquette for Love and Romance
Barbara Cartland's Book of Health

Cookery:
Barbara Cartland's Health Food Cookery Book
Food for Love
Magic of Honey Cookbook
Recipes for Lovers
The Romance of Food

Editor of:
"The Common Problem" by Ronald Cartland (with a preface by

the Rt. Hon. the Earl of Selborne, P.C.)
Barbara Cartland's Library of Love
Library of Ancient Wisdom

"Written with Love"
Passionate Love Letters selected by Barbara Cartland

Drama:
Blood Money
French Dressing

Philosophy:
Touch the Stars

Radio Operetta:
The Rose and the Violet (Music by Mark Lubbock) Performed in 1942

Radio Plays:
The Caged Bird: An episode in the life of Elizabeth Empress of Austria Performed in 1957

General:
Barbara Cartland's Book of Useless Information with a Foreword by the Earl Mountbatten of Burma.
(In aid of the United World Colleges)
Love and Lovers (Picture Book)
The Light of Love (Prayer Book)
Barbara Cartland's Scrapbook
(In aid of the Royal Photographic Museum)
Romantic Royal Marriages
Barbara Cartland's Book of Celebrities
Getting Older, Growing Younger

Verse:
Lines on Life and Love

Music:
An Album of Love Songs sung with the Royal Philharmonic Orchestra

Film:
The Flame is Love

Cartoons:
Barbara Cartland Romances (Book of Cartoons) has recently been published in the U.S.A., Great Britain, and other parts of the world.

Children:
A Children's Pop-Up Book: "Princess to the Rescue"

Barbara Cartland

An Angel Runs Away £1.95

When an aggrieved Marquis of Raventhorpe helped the runaway Ula into his carriage, she looked more like a tear-stained angel than the niece of the Earl of Chessington-Crewe and an instrument of revenge. For Ula, the Marquis turned a dream into reality, until the Earl, with sadistic cruelty, turned the tables. Dragged from a heaven of happiness to an attic in hell, Ula despaired that he would ever know she loved him, or could ever come to her rescue again.

Look With Love £1.75

After the death of her father, Ilitta is told by her aunt that she is now alone, unwanted and penniless and must therefore take employment under an assumed name with the Marchioness of Lyss who has been blinded in an accident. At Lyss Castle, Ilitta discovers the deep animosity which exists between the Marchioness and her stepson. Even as Ilitta rescues them both from a hell of hopelessness and despair, the knowledge of her aunt's threat overshadows her growing love for the Marquis. How could he ever marry someone who has behaved so very indiscreetly?

Love is a Gamble £1.75

Idona was horrified to learn that before her father was killed in a duel he had gambled away his house, his estate, and even herself to the Marquis of Wroxham. Her first unconventional meeting with this cynical dandy led to his introducing Idona to London society as his ward. Idona soon fled back to the country, bewildered by the intrigues and deceptions. Only when the Marquis followed did she realise that the turn of a card had won them the most precious prize in the world – love.

Barbara Cartland

Love Comes West £1.25

Roberta thought her adventures were over when she left Algiers to begin a new life in California. Yet there she met a sadistic preacher, a penniless painter, and an eccentric millionaire – not forgetting an orphan boy and hungry puppy. Her head often ruled her heart, but not when it came to posing for Adam and running away. When Adam's burning kisses sealed their reunion Roberta knew the light of love would shine from his every canvas.

Revenge of the Heart £1.95

Considering he had saved her from drowning, Nadia felt she had no option but to comply with Warren's request that she pose as his fiancée and accompany him to England. At Buckwood House new dangers threaten Nadia as she falls more and more in love with the Marquis. And only much later can she reveal the secrets of her past and seek new happiness in Warren's gentle kisses.

Love Joins the Clans £1.95

Penniless, with her mother dying of starvation, Clova faced the choice of either drowning or surrendering to the evils of nineteenth century Paris. Fortunately, the arrival of a Scottish elder brought the news that her father, chieftain of the clan of McBlane, was dead and that she now inherited the title. Warmly welcomed by both relatives and clansmen, Clova arouses the hatred of an envious cousin. With everything at stake, only one person could save her – the man who held her heart – and the McBlanes' bitterest enemy.

Barbara Cartland

Safe at Last £1.75

Otila Ashe was a wealthy young heiress, a tempting prize, and a man-hater. Desperate to escape from Paris and a menacing future she turned in her hour of need to Lord Kirkly, a confessed woman-hater. Pursued across the frontier into Italy by a vindictive fortune-seeking French family, they needed all their ingenuity to keep ahead. As her would-be captors closed in, Otila and Lord Kirkly found their answer in a love so compelling that they could only surrender to its divine power.

Temptation for a Teacher £1.75

Faced with the necessity of earning her own living, Lady Arletta Cherrington-Weir gladly impersonated a friend and went as a governess to the Dordogne. An atmosphere of menace and mystery surrounded the beautiful castle of Etienne, Duc de Sauterre. Known to have an obsessive hatred of things English, he was feared by everyone and even suspected of murder. Innocent victim of a wicked conspiracy, Arletta little thought that by falling in love with Etienne she was condemning them both to a watery grave.

All these books are available at your local bookshop or newsagent, or can be ordered direct from the publisher. Indicate the number of copies required and fill in the form below.

....

Name ____

(Block letters please)

Address ______________________________________

____

Send to CS Department, Pan Books Ltd, PO Box 40, Basingstoke, Hants
Please enclose remittance to the value of the cover price plus:
35p for the first book plus 15p per copy for each additional book ordered to a maximum charge of £1.25 to cover postage and packing
Applicable only in the UK

While every effort is made to keep prices low, it is sometimes necessary to increase prices at short notice. Pan Books reserve the right to show on cover and charge new retail prices which may differ from those advertised in the text or elsewhere